MOST MUSCULAR

Chris Levine

MOST MUSCULAR

First Edition: 2025

For more information, visit: onlychrislevine.com

CHAPTER I

The sultry sound of soft rock filled the dimly lit room, mingling with the heavy grunts and moans that rose in waves, matching the rhythm of the creaking bed. Sara's fingers dug into Adam's back, her breaths ragged and desperate.

"Oh, Adam," she gasped, her voice trembling as she neared the edge. "No one has ever made me feel this way."

Her words were raw, full of longing, but Adam barely heard them. His focus was elsewhere. With every thrust, his eyes flickered to the bedroom mirror, locking onto his own reflection. The dim light cast sharp shadows across his body, accentuating every line and to him, every single flaw.

Unaware of her partner's growing distance, Sara's moans grew louder, her body arching beneath him, but Adam's gaze lingered on the glass. Disappointment etched itself into his expression as his lips tightened. He looked away, only to glance back again, unable to stop himself. His movements became mechanical, disconnected, his mind a thousand miles away.

While Sara writhed beneath him, completely caught in the moment, Adam wasn't there anymore. The man in the mirror mocked him, every imperfection glaring back, louder than her cries of pleasure.

He leaned in closer, bringing his lips to her ear. "Do I

look big to you?"

"What? Yes—baby just don't stop, I'm so close!" Sara replied, her moans growing louder.

Adam tried to quicken his rhythm. Doing all he could to match her arousal, but the nagging thought in his mind about his body size derailed his focus and sapped his already waning libido.

As his disinterest peaked, he looked down in disgust at his deflated erection. He let out a frustrated, embarrassed groan and rolled off her, his body tense with defeat.

Sara laid next to him with the sheets partially covering the soft curves of her body, confused at the abrupt end to their lovemaking.

But Adam wasn't thinking about her. He was thinking about himself. More like looking at himself—his bare chest, his arms, his shoulders. Everything about him felt small.

His mind replayed those moments earlier in bed when he had felt confident for a few minutes but then, practically out of nowhere, that confidence slipped away, leaving this bitter taste of self-doubt. And no matter how much Sara tried to draw his attention back to her, he couldn't shake the feeling of inadequacy.

"Is it me?" Sara finally whispered to him.

He turned away from her without a word, rolling onto his side to avoid meeting her eyes. It was always him. He was the problem. Once again, he had let the moment slip through his fingers.

This wasn't the first time. That hollow, inadequate feeling had followed him for as long as he could remember, but lately, it had consumed him. For months now, the dysmorphia had been relentless, warping his perception until all he could see were flaws. No matter how much he tried to ignore it, his own body always found a way to ruin these moments with Sara.

And it wasn't just in bed; it was everywhere. The suffocating sense of being smaller, weaker, less-than was following him like a dark cloud heavy with rain. Sara could tell something was wrong, but she didn't know how to reach him.

Adam could be annoyingly stubborn when he wanted to be.

The next morning, Adam woke up earlier than usual, his body heavy with exhaustion. Sleep had been elusive, slipping through his grasp every time he closed his eyes. He hadn't just slept poorly—he'd barely slept at all.

He dragged his feet into the kitchen after grabbing a quick shower, and started making cereal. The sound of the spoon scraping against the bowl seemed deafening in the quiet house.

He heard Sara's soft footsteps but didn't turn around.

"Morning..." Sara said hesitantly, as if testing the waters.

"Hey—good morning..." Adam responded with a nod and a grim expression.

The silence between them hung heavy, awkward and unyielding. Adam could sense her searching for the right words to bridge the growing distance, but he wasn't in the mood to hear them. He didn't want to talk about last night or about anything, really. He didn't want to talk about another thing he was failing at.

"Adam, can we—?" Sara started, but before she could finish, Adam loudly dumped the bowl in the sink and grabbed his keys from the counter.

"I'm running late," he muttered. He walked out the door leaving a cold kiss on her cheek before she could say anything more.

The drive to work was no better. Every small bump added to his growing frustration—the slow traffic, the terrible drivers, and the damn cycling dudes in their stupid tight fitting outfits taking up the entire lane, all yanked at Adam's last good nerve. It was like the universe was working against him today. So by the time he got to work, he was already in a foul mood.

When he approached the office entrance, things only got more frustrating. The hulking security officer at the front, an African-American middle-aged woman with dark skin and darker eyes who always seemed to have a chip on her shoulder, gave Adam a slow long look before blocking his path and handing him a clipboard.

"I know you didn't just ignore the sign. You need to sign in," the guard said flatly, not moving from her spot.

"But I work here," Adam said through gritted teeth. The guard raised an eyebrow and snorted, clearly not caring. "Company policy, sir. Sign in."

This wasn't the day. Adam had enough.

"What the hell are you talking about? You've seen me come in almost everyday since you started working here." Adam scoffed frustratingly.

The big security woman just shrugged with a nasty smile on her face. She saw him as weak and wanted to take advantage.

Just then Mr. Thomas, a top-floor executive, walked up to the lobby entrance and glanced between both of them. He smelled of too much cologne and wore a million dollar smile.

"Morning Betsy, is this guy bothering you?" he asked.

"Oh good morning Mr. Thomas. He's not a problem sir. He just has to sign in and be on his way," Betsy said with a pointed look at Adam.

"Why the fuck should I sign in? I work here. You know I do—only guests have to sign in, I work in 401!" Adam shouted.

Mr. Thomas and Betsy burst out laughing at Adam's outburst.

"Don't work too hard Bets, good luck with 401 over here." Mr. Thomas said as he walked in without signing, leaving Betsy with a slow rub on her shoulder.

Adam felt a surge of anger from deep in his gut but gave in and signed-in anyway. He hated how easily he succumbed to the guard's antics. He hated how people treated him like he didn't belong. It wasn't just the stupid guard either.

Once inside office 401, the receptionist pointedly refused to acknowledge his presence, typing away at her computer as if he were invisible.

"Yeah good morning to you too," Adam mumbled to himself.

He continued toward his so-called desk—a cramped

cubicle indistinguishable from the endless sea of identical, gray partitions.

The chilly office buzzed with the droning hum of meaningless chatter, a symphony of monotony performed by worker ants, each burrowed in their little ant holes. Faces glowed faintly in the pale light of computer screens, void of any real expression, just blank stares and forced smiles. Every word exchanged felt hollow, like the people here spoke only to remind themselves they still existed. It was a hive of mediocrity, each ant scurrying to nowhere.

As Adam finally reached his cubicle and sank into his chair, hoping for just a fleeting moment of respite, his hopes were dashed by the unmistakable sound of heavy, labored breathing. Mr. Louis, his perpetually red-faced, beer-bellied boss, was waddling his way over, each step punctuated by a faint wheeze.

"Adam," Mr. Louis barked, his voice a grating mix of irritation and smug satisfaction. His tie was loosened, revealing a sweat-stained collar, and his beady eyes narrowed as he towered over the cubicle wall like a vulture eyeing its next meal.

"You know," he began, slapping a thick, calloused hand on the edge of Adam's desk, "these numbers of yours are embarrassing. Embarrassing! I'd be doing this place a favor by getting rid of you. You're lucky I have to deal with HR first."

Adam stiffened, gripping the edge of his desk to stop himself from saying anything reckless.

Mr. Louis leaned in closer, the smell of cheap coffee and stale cigarettes on his breath. "You've got one week—one—to pull your head out of your ass, or I swear, Adam, I'll have the pleasure of showing you the door myself. Maybe flipping burgers is more your speed, huh? Less thinking required."

Without waiting for a reply, Mr. Louis straightened up, his belly jiggling slightly, and waddled off to torment someone else, muttering about "useless employees" under his breath. Adam sat frozen, his stomach churning as the echoes of Louis's rant lingered in the air, a cruel reminder that even here, there was no peace.

He couldn't help but wonder if the shit conditions at work was his own doing. Was his frustration showing? Or was it something else, something about his appearance that made people treat him this way?

After enduring Mr. Louis' loud, demeaning tirade, Adam barely had time to collect himself before a tall, athletic black man strolled up to his cubicle named George. His tailored suit fit like a glove, exuding effortless style, and his easy, confident smile seemed to brighten the dreary office.

George was Adam's only real ally in the entire office—and, if he was honest, his closest friend outside of work too. They went way back, all the way to high school. George had been the star athlete, the guy everyone wanted to be: charming, popular, and seemingly good at everything. Adam had been the "smart kid," the one teachers adored and classmates relied on for help. Despite their differences, they clicked, forging a bond that had outlasted the petty cliques and labels of their teenage years.

"Man," George said, leaning casually on the side of Adam's cubicle, "Louis really knows how to start the day off right, doesn't he? You good?"

Adam glanced up at him, managing a faint smile. George always had a way of cutting through the noise, his presence a reminder that not everyone in this place sucked.

"Yeah—I just zone him out." Adam shifted uncomfortably in his chair.

"Well that shit was foul, Mr. Louis knows better than to talk that ish to me—I'd fu—"

Adam looked up at George interrupting him,
"Hey man do I look big to you?"

"Uhh define big," George, caught off guard, answered quickly, then immediately finished his sentence.

"But yeah—I'd fuck him up he talk to me like that!" Looking out into the office as if he was saying it to Mr. Louis himself.

"Hey, I'm serious man." Adam replied.

George sized him up. "I mean you could put on a few more pounds. I am naturally blessed so I don't need to work out, some aren't."

George playfully pointed at Adam.

"Thanks," Adam muttered, his voice tinged with frustration. He turned back to his computer, clearly trying to brush George off.

"Hey, man," George said, undeterred. "Who cares if you're not built like a bodybuilder? You've got a smoking-hot fiancé, and that's all that matters."

As he spoke, George casually reached over and picked up a framed photo of Adam and Sara from the desk. He tilted it, studying it with a playful grin. "No offense, but there's no way you're hitting that right my dude!"

Adam's face darkened instantly. He snatched the picture out of George's hands, his grip firm and his jaw tight. "You can leave now, George. I should get back to work."

"Relax. I'm just kidding!" George replied, holding his hands up in mock surrender.

He stepped back, still grinning.

"We cool right?"

Adam sighed, forcing himself to soften slightly. "Yeah–we're cool."

"My man, see ya at lunch." George smiled and as he turned to leave, launched into an exaggerated impression of Mr. Louis. He puffed out his chest, slapped his stomach, and bellowed,

"Now make those sales numbers go up, or else—"

Adam watched him go, his grin faltering as he glanced at the picture still clutched in his hand. Gently, he set it back down on his desk, staring at it for a moment longer before turning his attention back to his screen.

The thought of George telling him he wasn't fucking Sara right gnawed at him all morning. He tried to make a few calls but ultimately just sat quietly at his desk, allowing his mind to roam far into places it shouldn't.

As hours passed Adam just stared at his monitor, ignoring the blinking cursor in his work software. He was done making calls, done pretending to care about quotas. Instead, he opened his browser and typed in a phrase that had been gnawing at him for months: how to build muscle fast.

The screen lit up with a cascade of results—articles, fitness blogs, and step-by-step workout routines. But what grabbed his attention wasn't the advice. It was the ads. Bold, colorful banners plastered across the page screamed promises of instant transformation using one word: steroids—the shortcut of shortcuts. Each one dangled the same tantalizing reward: a bigger, stronger, better body.

Adam leaned back in his chair, his mind spinning. Was this the answer? Was this what he needed to feel like himself again—or someone better? He shook his head, dismissing the impulse, and instead slammed the browser shut. Frustration bubbled in his chest as he stared at the blank screen. The fact that he'd even entertained the idea made his stomach churn. It wasn't who he was—was it?

At lunch, George unwrapped a sandwich, the smell of deli meat and mustard filling the air, while Adam absentmindedly munched on a bag of chips.

"Yo! That's your lunch?" George said, laughing as he gestured at Adam's sad snack.

"What? I'm not really hungry," Adam replied with a shrug.

George shook his head, grinning. "Man, how are you gonna ask me if I think you're big when you're out here eating a bag of chips for lunch? You gotta eat, dawg!"

Ignoring the jab, Adam blurted out, "Do you know anything about steroids?"

George froze mid-bite, eyebrows shooting up. "Steroids? Nah, black people don't mess with that stuff, man." Adam gave him a skeptical look.

"What are you talking about? Ever heard of Barry Bonds?"

George waved his sandwich dismissively.

"Alright, yeah, him. But he's one of the few. That stuff was invented for white guys like you trying to keep up with us brothers."

"Okay, sure," Adam muttered, rolling his eyes. "But seriously, do you know anything about them?"

George leaned back, chewing thoughtfully.

"I knew a dude in college who used them. Had to shoot it in his ass, man. Dude could barely sit down most of the time. Always walking funny. Why? You thinking about juicing?"

"No–no, I hate needles–I get queasy just giving blood," Adam said quickly.

George smirked, pointing at him with half a sandwich.

"Good. My advice. Learn to work out for real and get on some kind of eating schedule. You know, with actual food."

"Yeah, okay. True," Adam said, nodding. He straightened up a little. "You know what? I'm going to start today. Hit the gym, eat better, all of it."

"Yeah? Good for you, bro!" George said, grinning wide. "Oh, and that Mr. Louis nonsense earlier? Forget about it. You'd have to do something really dumb to get fired from this place. Here." He slid a wrapped sandwich across the table. "Take my other one. You gotta eat if you want to get big."

Adam hesitated before taking the sandwich, peeling back the wrapper.

"Thanks for lunch, George," he said, taking a bite.

"No problem, man," George said, smirking. "Now go get those gains bro."

After work, Adam changed into the spare clothes he kept in his car and drove to the local gym, Titan Fitness. The place was alive with activity, the hum of treadmills and the rhythmic clanging of weights blending into a constant roar. The smell of sweat and rubber filled the air, a mix that was both energizing and intimidating.

He made his way to a bench press tucked into a corner, hoping to avoid too much attention. Sliding under the bar, he gripped it tightly and took a deep breath. It was just the bar—no weights added—but as he pushed it up, it felt heavier than he expected. His arms trembled, struggling to stabilize it.

With every shaky rep, frustration built. He pushed harder, gritting his teeth, but his arms finally gave out. The bar came crashing down onto his chest, pinning him in place. Adam gasped, his face turning red as he scrambled to free himself, the sting of failure hitting harder than the weight ever could.

A massive bodybuilder walking by noticed Adam's struggle and stepped in without hesitation.

"Need a spot?" the guy asked, effortlessly lifting the bar off Adam's chest like it weighed nothing.

Adam nodded, too embarrassed and out of breath to answer. The man's muscles rippled as he set the barbell back on the rack. For a brief moment, Adam let himself imagine looking like that—broad, powerful, almost godlike. But the vision felt impossibly distant, more fantasy than reality.

"Thanks, man—I had it, though," Adam said, his pride forcing the words out.

The bodybuilder chuckled, an easy smile on his face.

"I know you did. Just let me know if you need a spot next time. Name's Jason." He extended a thick hand, his grip firm but friendly, and left after their quick introduction.

Adam sat up, staring at the empty barbell. He laid back down, ready to give it another shot, but hesitated. Instead, he sat up again, rubbing his shoulder in an exaggerated motion as if trying to telegraph to anyone watching that it wasn't his strength holding him back—just an old injury acting up. But when he glanced around, no one was looking.

He stood and wandered over to the treadmill section, reluctantly climbing onto one and starting at a slow walk. As his feet moved mechanically, his eyes roamed the gym, taking in all the people who seemed to be leagues ahead of him—fit, confident, in control.

His sour mood clung to him like a shadow, stubborn and unshakable. It had followed him from the office to the gym, and now, as he trudged back to his car and drove home, it stayed with him still, a constant reminder of how far he felt from the man he wanted to be.

He arrived home, barely sparing a second to Sara, who was putting away groceries in the kitchen. He headed straight for the bathroom, closing the door behind him.

In the quiet, Adam felt himself unraveling. The mirror stared back at him again, that same reflection that haunted him earlier. His body, scrawnier than he was before the gym, seemed to mock him. He felt trapped inside it, like no matter how hard he tried, it would never change fast enough.

Sitting on the edge of the bathtub, Adam stared at his phone, desperate for an escape from the mounting frustration and feelings of inadequacy. His thoughts drifted to fleeting fantasies, momentary reprieves from the weight he couldn't seem to shake. Succumbing to the urge, he searched for porn, hoping the rush of release would offer some kind of relief.

Minutes passed as he scrolled aimlessly, trying to find something that stirred even the faintest arousal. But nothing clicked. Nothing worked. His body refused to cooperate, leaving him more frustrated than before.

"God damn it!" Adam shouted, his voice echoing in the small bathroom.

"Adam?" Sara's voice came from the other side of the door, gentle but laced with concern. "Are you okay in there, honey?"

"Yeah, I'm fine," he muttered, wiping a hand across his face. But he knew she didn't believe him.

"Can I come in?" she asked softly, her tone almost pleading.

"No!" Adam snapped, the sharpness of his voice surprising even himself. He instantly regretted it but couldn't bring himself to apologize. "Don't come in. I'll be out shortly."

Silence lingered for a few minutes before Adam finally unlocked the door and stepped out, brushing past Sara without a word. She stood there, frozen, hurt flashing across her face as she watched him retreat down the hallway.

Left alone, Sara slowly made her way back to the kitchen, her heart heavy with the weight of their unspoken problems. She picked up her phone, her fingers trembling slightly as she dialed. The line clicked, and her good friend Anne's familiar voice came through.

"Hey, Sara. Howdy."

"Hey, Anne," Sara replied, her tone immediately betraying her emotions.

"What's the matter?" Anne asked, her voice softening.

Sara glanced over her shoulder, making sure Adam wasn't nearby. "I don't know what to do anymore," she whispered urgently. "Adam just... he won't talk to me. He shuts down, and it's affecting everything." She hesitated, her voice breaking slightly. "Even our sex life. It's like he's not even here anymore. His body won't even respond to me, Anne."

Anne's tone became more serious, yet still comforting. "It sounds like he's going through something. Have you tried asking him about it?"

"Of course I've tried," Sara said, her voice trembling as tears welled up. "But it's like he's closed off. He can't even stay, you know–hard anymore. Do you think he's just–not attracted to me anymore?"

Unbeknownst to her, Adam was standing just outside the kitchen, his heart sinking with every word. Hearing Sara's pain—and the brutal honesty about his own struggles—hit him like a gut punch. He hadn't meant for things to spiral this far out of control. Yet here they were, their lives unraveling piece by piece, crumbling under the weight of everything they couldn't hold together, and he had no idea how to stop it from falling apart completely.

CHAPTER 2

Adam woke up with a jolt, his body drenched in cold sweat. The nightmares had felt so real, still lingering in the corners of his mind. They replayed every silly and not-so-silly fear he had about his life—his appearance, his job, his deteriorating relationship with Sara.

His heart pounded in his chest as he tried to catch his breath. He stretched out his hand till he could touch Sara, who was peacefully asleep beside him.

He envied her peaceful sleep, her ability to rest without the weight of crippling anxiety crushing her. Adam sighed deeply and wiped his forehead with the back of his hand. Why couldn't he shake this stupid feeling?

He looked back to the ceiling, still searching for sleep but unfortunately could not find any.

Everything still felt off. His body was painfully scrawny, his colleagues treated him like a doormat, and his future loomed ahead, emptier and more uncertain than ever.

Adam wanted to scream his lungs raw into his pillow, but instead, he just lay there, wrapped in the quiet darkness of their bedroom. Frustration and a growing sense of failing were his only companions.

The next morning, Adam dragged himself back to work, moving on autopilot for most of the day. He sat in his cubicle and stared blankly at his computer screen. His fingers rested on the mouse but not clicking. The exhaustion from the nightmare and mostly sleepless night clung to him, making the office feel even more suffocating than usual.

He rubbed his tired eyes repeatedly and tried to focus, putting on his headset to make the daily calls he had grown to loathe.

His job in telemarketing was draining. He had gotten used to the rude responses and endless rejection, but now it just felt like a dead end. No matter how many hours he worked, no matter how many damn calls he placed, it never seemed like enough.

Just as Adam was about to dial the next number, his cell phone buzzed on the desk. "Mom" flashed across the screen.

He hesitated, glancing around the office to ensure no one was close enough to eavesdrop. Sliding off his headset, he tossed it onto the desk with little care and picked up the call.

"Hey, mom," Adam said, his voice low.

"Hi, honey! How are you?" his mother's familiar warmth radiated through the phone, though it only made Adam shift uncomfortably in his chair.

"Uhm, alright, I guess. I'm kinda—"

"I know, I know. You're busy," she cut in, her tone light but firm, like she had anticipated his answer. "Listen, I'm making dinner tonight. Why don't you and Sara come by?"

Adam frowned, his free hand rubbing the back of his neck. "Mom, it's not really a good time. Work's been... stressful. And things with Sara—well, they're a little off right now."

"Just a quick dinner," she urged, breezing past his excuses. "We haven't seen you in weeks. Are you avoiding us?"

Adam's jaw tightened at the question. She wasn't wrong, but he wasn't ready to admit it. Silence hung between them as he searched for the right words.

"Good, then it's settled," she said, her decision final

before he could argue. "Tonight at 7. Love you!"

"Bye, Mom," Adam muttered before the line clicked off.

He stared at the phone for a moment, an uneasy weight settling in his chest. Glancing around the office, he quickly grabbed his headset and slid it back on, forcing himself to return to the drudgery of calls. But the interruption lingered. He already knew how the night would go: forced smiles, awkward conversations, and the gnawing sense that it would only leave him feeling worse.

That evening, Adam and Sara pulled up outside his parents' house. The drive had been quiet with both of them lost in their own thoughts. Sara, holding a bottle of red wine, didn't say much, but the tension between them was palpable. They felt more like strangers than a couple these days.

Adam knocked on the door, mentally preparing himself for what was to come. Moments later, his father, Bob Stenson, opened the door with a wide grin.

Bob was a big man, with a big spirit. He had salt and pepper hair and tanned skin. Bob was full of life, a nearly restless bundle of energy. He practically exploded out of the door.

"Hey, son! How are ya?" Bob asked, his voice booming with his trademark confidence Adam had always envied but never quite understood.

"Hey, dad. I'm good, thanks," Adam replied, though the smile didn't quite reach his eyes.

Bob turned his attention to Sara. "Hi, Sara. You look as beautiful as always."

"Thank you, Mr. Stenson," Sara said politely, though her tone was a bit distant.

"Now, how many times do I have to tell you? It's Bob," he laughed, stepping aside to let them in. "Come in, your mother's still cooking."

They walked inside, the familiar smell of lasagna and garlic bread filling the air. But instead of feeling comforted, Adam felt a knot form in his stomach—this dinner was going to be anything but pleasant.

The dining room was set, though the food wasn't on the table yet. Bob pulled out a chair for Sara, who sat down with a small smile. Adam's mother called from the kitchen, her voice warm and inviting, though he knew better than to think tonight would be easy.

"Dinner's almost ready! Adam, come help your mom please." she called.

Adam stood reluctantly and headed to the kitchen, where his mother was pulling the garlic bread from the oven. The smell was comforting and nostalgic, reminding him of a simpler time in his childhood.

"Hi, mom," Adam said as he entered, walking over to give her a hug. She hugged him back, holding on just a bit too long. His mom, Catherine Stenson was a small woman who always smelled like perfumes. She was warm and beautiful with bouncy black hair and soft grey eyes.

"I missed you honey," she said, looking him over. "You look great, Adam. Work is good?"

Adam shrugged. "Yeah, it's fine. I'm surviving."

His mother's gaze shifted toward the dining room where Sara sat. "And how is she?" she asked, clearly fishing for more information.

Adam sighed, his patience wearing thin. "Good. Everything's fine."

"I know you, Adam. Everything isn't fine—"

"Mom, not tonight. Okay?" Adam interrupted, his voice firmer than he intended. He didn't want to talk about it, especially not here, not now.

His mother gave him a soft smile, but there was a hint of sadness in her eyes. "I'm just being your mother. A mother's job is never done, you know."

From the dining room, Bob's voice echoed through the house. "Leave our son alone! Let's eat!"

His mom smiled again and held up her hand, showing her wedding ring.

"Marriage," she said simply before handing him the lasagna dish. Adam grabbed it without a word, and they headed back to the dining room.

Dinner kicked off awkwardly. The tension between Adam and Sara hadn't gone unnoticed by his parents, but no one said anything outright. Bob poured the wine as they all sat down, trying to fill the silence with casual conversation.

"So, what have you two been doing now that you're retired?" Sara asked, trying to keep things light.

His mother laughed softly. "I hate to say it, but sleeping in and watching morning TV just doesn't get boring, does it, Bob?"

Bob muttered something under his breath, clearly frustrated by the monotony of retirement.

"What was that?" Catherine asked, raising an eyebrow.

"Nothing. It's great," Bob replied sarcastically.

"I need to figure out something to do. Maybe start my own business," Bob continued, more to himself than to anyone else. "There are these valves that buses use to open and close the air brakes. I have an idea—"

"Dad," Adam cut in, unable to hide his irritation. "You've been talking about that for years. Either do it or think of another idea."

Sara placed her hand on Adam's arm, trying to calm him. "Babe, let him—"

"No, it's fine," Bob said, though Adam could see the hurt in his eyes. "I can have my dream, alright. How's telemarketing treating you? Saving any money yet?"

Adam felt a flush of anger. "It's hard to save when you don't make much," he muttered.

"Should've gone for a county job," Bob said, shaking his head. "Good pay and benefits."

"Bob, stop it," his mother interjected, trying to keep the peace. "Let's just enjoy our meal."

Sara smiled. "It's really good."

"Thank you, hun. It's actually store-bought," his mother replied with a hearty laugh. "I'm sorry, I can't cook. Never have."

"Do you think that's why Adam stays skinny?" Sara asked, teasing.

"I'm not skinny," Adam snapped, suddenly feeling defensive.

"I mean lean," Sara corrected herself, trying to keep the joke light.

Bob chuckled. "Always told that boy to eat more growing up."

"Well, Adam was a picky eater," his mother added. "Couldn't get him to finish a meal."

Adam felt his temper rise. "Maybe I wasn't a picky eater. Maybe I just didn't like the way your food tasted."

His mother's face fell, the tension at the table thickening. The laughter faded, and for a moment, no one spoke.

"Let's just enjoy this meal as a family," his mother said quietly, her voice strained.

They ate the rest of their meal in silence after that, each of them pretending that the evening hadn't just gone completely off course.

Later that night, as Adam and Sara got back to their apartment, the awkwardness between them was even more apparent. The drive home had been silent, both of them too exhausted to even try to make conversation.

"I'm going to take a shower," Sara said as she walked toward the bathroom. She glanced over her shoulder, offering a weak smile. "Want to join me?"

It was a half-hearted attempt to rekindle something between them and Adam loved her for trying. But he wasn't in the mood. The dinner conversation still lingered in his mind, and he couldn't shake the frustration building inside him.

"The gym is still open," Adam replied, checking the time. "I'm going to get a quick workout in."

Sara didn't look surprised. In fact, she barely reacted at all. "I'm actually feeling tired anyway," she said softly, turning away. She reached for her phone and buried her nose in it.

Adam headed to the bedroom to change into his gym clothes, the silence in the apartment heavy. As he pulled on his workout gear, Sara stood alone in the hallway, her phone in her hand. She stared at the screen for a moment, her thumb hovering over a name in her contacts list.

CHAPTER 3

The cold night air nipped at Adam's skin as he walked towards the gym. He drew in a deep breath, letting the crisp air fill his lungs, trying to push away the frustrations of the day. Tonight, he was determined to focus on his workout, hoping the rhythmic strain of lifting weights might quiet the chaos in his mind.

The gym was quickly becoming Adam's sanctuary, a place where he could sweat out his insecurities and silence the noise in his head.

The brightly lit space greeted him with the sharp, metallic scent of iron and the faint musk of sweat. The clanking of weights and the dull hum of treadmills filled the air, a familiar symphony that made him feel grounded. He headed to the front desk to check in.

At the counter stood the stereotypical gym alpha—a broad-shouldered guy with bulging muscles, an inflated sense of self-importance, and a swagger that screamed ego overload. His overly tanned skin had a slight reddish hue, the kind that screamed water retention from something stronger than creatine, and his ridiculous faux-hawk only added to the caricature.

He was deep in conversation with the girl behind the desk, who seemed far more invested in their chat than in her actual job.

"I don't know, I got so drunk last night," she giggled, twirling a strand of her hair around her finger.

Adam stood there, waiting awkwardly, his patience slipping away with every tick of the clock. He shifted his weight from one foot to the other, glancing around, hoping they'd notice him. Finally, he cleared his throat.

"Umm, excuse me—" Adam said, his voice tentative.

The gym bro turned around sharply, his face darkening as though Adam had just interrupted something critical. He stared at Adam with a mix of disdain and irritation.

"Hey, bro, relax. Can't you see we're talking?" the guy said, his tone dripping with condescension.

Adam's face burned as humiliation mixed with anger, but he didn't want to start a scene. He just wanted to check in and get his workout over with.

"Yeah—sorry, just want to check in, man," Adam mumbled, his voice quieter, his eyes dropping to the floor.

The gym bro smirked, flexing slightly as he turned back to the desk, running his hand through his awkward mohawk. "I just want to check in," he mocked in a whiny tone. Then, with a smirk, he added, "Those five-pound dumbbell curls aren't getting you anywhere, man."

The front desk girl finally acknowledged Adam, her tone flat and uninterested. "Do you have your key tag?" she asked, as though this entire exchange was the greatest inconvenience of her day.

Adam handed it over, careful not to make eye contact as his fingers brushed against hers. She scanned it and slid it back to him without a second glance.

"Enjoy your workout, man," the gym bro added, the sarcasm practically dripping from his words as he watched Adam walk away.

Adam kept his head down, his face burning with humiliation. The interaction left him feeling small, like he didn't belong here, like he never would. As he made his way to the weight racks, he forced himself to focus. He couldn't let a muscle-headed idiot derail him. He came here for a reason.

He needed to stick to it.

At the dumbbell rack, Adam's eyes scanned the neatly arranged weights until they landed on a pair of 15-pound dumbbells. He picked them up, the heft settling in his hands. With slow, deliberate movements, he began curling, focusing intently on each rep, every contraction of his biceps. By the tenth repetition, he set the dumbbells down and flexed his arms slightly, relishing the faint "pump" building in his muscles. It reminded him of something Arnold once described in the movie Pumping Iron.

Out of the corner of his eye, he noticed someone nearby. A girl, effortlessly curling a pair of 15-pound dumbbells with perfect form. She didn't seem to struggle at all, her movements smooth and controlled. Adam's confidence wavered. Was he really lifting the same weight as her?

His jaw tightened as he placed the dumbbells back on the rack. Without giving himself time to think, he grabbed a pair of 20-pound weights. His pride demanded it, driving him to prove he was stronger, better, more capable.

The added weight strained his arms immediately, but he clenched his teeth and pushed through, counting each rep in his head. He needed to do this. He needed to be better. Stronger. Bigger.

After finishing his dumbbell curls, Adam made his way to the machine area. It was the part of the gym typically occupied by older folks and the so-called casuals, but he didn't care. His arms were burning from the 20-pound curls, and besides, he had developed a fondness for the bicep curling machine. He adjusted the seat and settled in.

As he started his set, his eyes wandered to the machine beside him, where an older woman was working out. She noticed him and offered a warm, friendly smile. Adam hesitated, forcing a half-hearted smile in return before quickly looking away, his stomach twisting. In his mind, everyone in the gym was silently laughing at him, sizing him up and finding him lacking.

He shook the thought off and refocused on the machine, gripping the handles tightly. With each rep, he pushed harder, his muscles straining under the weight. He wanted to prove to himself that he wasn't just another skinny guy floundering in a place filled with people stronger and more capable than him.

Giving up wasn't an option. This wasn't just about fitness; it felt like survival—building muscle or die trying. But the truth of it hit harder than the weights. It was grueling, unforgiving, and far more difficult than Adam had imagined.
After finishing on the machine, Adam found himself standing in front of the gym mirrors that covered an entire wall, his eyes locked on his reflection.

He pulled up his shirt slightly, flexing his arms, inspecting his biceps. They looked bigger—at least, he thought they did. But as he stood there, admiring his modest progress, a bodybuilder stepped up next to him.

The man's muscles were enormous and perfectly defined, his veins bulging out of his skin as he flexed confidently in front of the mirror. He was the epitome of strength and power, everything Adam wanted to be but wasn't.

Adam glanced at the bodybuilder's reflection, feeling a pang of jealousy and more than a little insecurity. The bodybuilder, oblivious to Adam's internal struggle, continued flexing, his muscles rippling under the gym lights.

Unable to bear the comparison any longer, Adam quickly walked away, frustrated at his lack of progress, his heart heavy with disappointment.

As he left the gym, Adam passed the front desk girl again. She was busy saying goodbye to other members, her smile bright and cheerful. But when it came to Adam, she didn't even acknowledge him, her gaze sliding right past him as if he didn't exist. Her refusal to acknowledge him stung, but Adam kept walking, his mind already elsewhere.

Adam unlocked the door to his apartment, stepping inside with his gym bag slung over his shoulder. The apartment was quiet, the dim lighting adding to the heavy atmosphere. As he dropped his bag near the door, he thought he heard a man's voice coming from the bedroom.

His heart raced, adrenaline surging through him. He quickly moved to the bedroom, running through multiple possibilities—each worse than the last.

Adam pushed the door open to find Sara standing by the window, her back turned to him. She spun around with a guilty look on her face, as if she had been caught in the act.

"Adam, what's wrong?" she asked, her voice deceptively calm.

"I thought I heard a voice," Adam said. He glanced past her toward the open window, his pulse still racing.

"Oh, I was on speaker with a friend," Sara explained, her tone light but not quite convincing.

"A male friend?" Adam questioned.

"What? No." she replied.

Adam's gaze shifted to the window again. "Why is the window open, then?"

Sara shrugged nonchalantly.

"Just letting in the night breeze. Is everything alright, honey?"

Adam was confused, the tension between them already thick in the air. He wanted to press further, to ask her who she had been talking to, but something held him back. Maybe it was the exhaustion from the gym, or maybe it was the growing distance between them that made him feel like the truth didn't matter anymore.

"Yeah, I'm fine," he finally said, his voice lacking conviction. "It's just —never mind. I'm going to jump in the shower."

Sara nodded, turning away from him.

"Okay, I'm going to bed. I have a lot to do tomorrow." Adam paused for a moment, watching her. He didn't want the night to end like this, with this gaping divide between them.

"I was thinking you could take a shower with me?" he asked, his voice hopeful.

Sara looked at him, her expression apologetic but

firm. "Sorry, babe. I already showered."

"Oh," Adam muttered, the rejection stinging more than he wanted to admit.

Sara offered him a small smile as she pulled back the covers on the bed.

"Good night." She leaned over and kissed him briefly before lying down and turning off the light.

Adam stood frozen for a moment, her words replaying in his mind like a broken record. Each syllable seemed to grow heavier, pressing down on his chest. The sting of rejection clung to him, mingling with an overwhelming sense of inadequacy. He turned toward the bathroom, his steps slow, dragging as if the weight of the moment had drained the strength from his body.

When he finally reached the bathroom, he stepped inside and shut the door behind him. He leaned against it, letting the cool surface press into his back as he closed his eyes. His breath came out in a long, shaky exhale, but it didn't bring the relief he was hoping for.

Adam opened his eyes and caught his reflection in the mirror. His shoulders slumped, his posture weak and defeated. The person staring back at him looked nothing like the man he wanted to be—no confidence, no strength, just a scrawny frame and tired eyes.

He pushed himself off the door and stepped closer to the sink, gripping the edges of the counter so hard his knuckles turned white. His mind raced, every thought circling back to the same questions. Why wasn't he enough? And why couldn't he be the kind of man who commanded respect, who looked and felt strong?

The next day at work, the steady hum of computers and the scattered chatter of colleagues hustling to close sales faded into the background. Adam sat at his desk, his focus locked on his screen. Instead of work-related spreadsheets, his browser was filled with bodybuilding websites. He clicked through page after page, devouring every article he could find about steroids.

His eyes darted over the words, carefully soaking in the information. Terms like deca, d-bol, and tren jumped off the screen, sparking a growing sense of curiosity. Steroids had always been a distant, almost forbidden concept—something he'd heard about but never truly considered. Yet now, for the first time, the idea seemed real, tangible. Maybe they were the solution to everything. Maybe they could turn him into the man he wanted to be—the man he needed to be.

As he scrolled further, one particular post caught his attention. The title read, "How to make your own finaplix." Adam's heart skipped a beat as he clicked on the thread. The page loaded with detailed instructions, diagrams, and step-by-step guides.

"I can make my own steroids?" he muttered under his breath, his thoughts spinning. The idea seemed wild, risky—but also thrilling. The gears in his head began to turn, curiosity giving way to a dangerous excitement.

He leaned closer to the screen, completely absorbed in the text, until a shadow loomed over his desk.

"Adam!"

The sudden bark of his boss, Mr. Louis, made him jump. He whipped around in his seat to find the red-faced, beer-bellied man glaring at him.

"What the hell are you doing?" Louis snapped, his eyes narrowing as he caught a glimpse of the browser. "Last I checked, we don't pay you to surf the damn web!"

Adam scrambled to close the tab, his hands fumbling over the mouse.

"I—I was just taking a quick break," he stammered, his voice barely above a whisper.

Mr. Louis snorted, his face twisting into a smug grin. "A break? You don't need a break—you need results."

He stopped mid-sentence, his eyes narrowing as he glanced at Adam's screen. A smirk tugged at his lips as he pointed at it and scoffed.

"So get back to work, or I swear, you'll be out of here faster than you can say the word... bodybuilding."

Leaning in slightly, his voice dipped into something colder, more cutting.

"Not that it matters for you Mr. Stenson. I've been lifting for years—probably too late for you anyway."

Adam nodded quickly, his face burning with humiliation. As Louis waddled away, muttering something under his breath, Adam stared at the now-empty screen. His heart was still racing, his mind a mess of shame and intrigue. The interruption hadn't dampened his curiosity—it had only made him more determined to explore the possibility.

Adam placed the cheap plastic headset back on, found a number from his leads list and dialed. As the phone rang, Adam glanced over at Mr. Louis, who was watching him like a hawk. Adam forced a polite smile as the call connected.

"Hello, sir, my name is Adam and I was wondering if you had a few minutes–"

"Stop calling me!" a man's voice shouted from the other end of the line, the sound so loud that Adam instinctively pulled the headset away from his ear.

Adam sighed, rubbing his temples as he hung up the phone. He glanced around the office, making sure Mr. Louis wasn't watching him anymore, and quickly reopened the minimized tab.

His eyes scanned the screen again, this time with more determination. "How to make finaplix." He began taking notes, writing down a list of supplies he would need and placed the order for the main ingredient, finaplix pellets.

As the distance between Adam and Sara grew wider, and after enduring a string of weak, humiliating workouts, the package finally arrived—a package that, in Adam's mind, would change his life forever.

He opened the front door, his eyes darting around

the empty hallway before snatching the box up and hurrying inside. His heart pounded, a mix of exhilaration and nerves coursing through him as he set it down on the counter.

In front of him sat the list he had carefully compiled, now matched by the contents of the box. Finaplix pellets. Syringes. Needle tips. Alcohol wipes. Coffee filters. Gloves. It was all there, the tools of transformation spread out like an altar of reinvention.

Adam took a deep, shaky breath, his fingers brushing over the instructions he had printed out. He read them again, his eyes scanning the precise steps as he steadied himself for what was to come. This was it. This was the solution. The way out of his weakness, his inadequacy. The way to finally become the man he'd always wanted to be.

With trembling hands, he began. Carefully, methodically, he followed each step. Crushing the pellets, dissolving them, filtering the solution—it all felt surreal, like a ritual more than a task. The sharp chemical smell of the process filled the air, but Adam hardly noticed. His mind was elsewhere, running wild with fantasies of the future.

He pictured himself walking into the gym, the heads of his colleagues and that smug gym dude turning in surprise as they gawked at his transformed physique. He imagined their envy, their shock, the respect they'd finally give him. He imagined Sara's eyes lighting up when she saw him, the admiration returning to her gaze, the distance between them melting away. She wouldn't doubt him anymore. She wouldn't pull back.

By the time the process was complete, Adam held a small vial of golden brown liquid in his hands, the culmination of his desperation and determination. He lifted it to the light, a smile creeping onto his face.

This was it. This was the key to everything. Blast off time.

Adam stood in front of the bathroom mirror, a syringe filled with golden brown liquid in his hand. His reflection stared back at him, a bit of fear and determination in his eyes.

"You can do this," Adam whispered to himself, his voice shaky.

He had already drawn the solution into the syringe. Now came the hard part—injecting it.

Adam pulled down his pants, exposing his butt cheek as he positioned the needle over the top section. His hand trembled slightly as he pushed the needle into his skin, the sharp sting making him wince.

"It's fine," he muttered to himself, trying to stay calm. But as he began to plunge the thick solution into his muscle, the pain became unbearable. The liquid wasn't moving through the needle as smoothly as he had hoped, and the needle itself started to shift around in his flesh.

Adam's face paled as he looked up at the mirror, his vision swimming. His heart pounded in his chest, panic rising as he felt the room start to spin. Before he knew it, everything went black.

Adam slowly came to, his head throbbing and his vision blurry. He was lying on the bathroom floor, his body cold against the tile. The needle was still sticking out of his ass and his bathroom counter was littered with syringes, alcohol wipes, vials.

"Adam!" Sara's voice broke through the fog in his mind. She was standing in the bathroom doorway, her face pale with shock as she took in the scene in front of her.

"Oh my god! What—what is this? What have you done?!"

Adam groaned, pulling the needle out of his skin, the sharp pain making him wince.

"Calm down," Adam muttered, his voice weak. "It's not what it looks like."

"Not what it looks like?" Sara cried, her voice rising in panic. "There are needles everywhere, and you were passed out on the floor with a needle sticking out of your ass! Are you doing drugs now? Is that fucking heroin?"

Adam shook his head, trying to sit up. "No, it's not heroin. It's a–." Adam tried to find the words...

"It's what Adam? What the fuck is that?!"

Adam searched for the words while still coming to his senses.

"Tell me now!"

Adam fired back without thinking.

"It's finaplix!"

Sara blinked, clearly not understanding.

"What the hell is finaplix?"

"It's steroids Sara, just steroids," Adam admitted, his voice barely above a whisper. "I was trying to inject it."

Sara stared at him, her eyes wide with disbelief.

"Steroids? Are you serious? Why? Why would you do this?"

Adam sighed, running a hand through his hair.

"I just—I want to put on some muscle. I want to look better, feel better. And I thought this would help. I'll be fine, I don't want you to worry about it."

"Don't you tell me not to worry about this! Steroids? Really? It's going to make your dick shrink and you are going to get fuckin' mean!"

"It doesn't make your dick shrink..." Adam replied.

"I'm not getting involved in this. I'm not doing this!"

Sara shook her head, tears welling up in her eyes.

"Adam, this is dangerous. You can't just inject yourself with steroids and expect it to fix everything. What about our wedding? What if this messes with your health? What if something happens to you?"

Adam stood up slowly, his legs shaky. He reached out and gently took her hand. "I'm going to be fine, I promise. This is just what I need. It's going to help solve all of our problems."

For a moment, Sara hesitated, her eyes searching his face for any sign of the man she used to know. Finally, she sighed and wrapped her arms around him.

"I just don't want you to get hurt," she whispered, her voice soft.

Adam hugged her back, feeling the tension between them start to melt away. He leaned down and kissed her gently, his hand resting on the small of her back.

"I'm not going to get hurt," Adam whispered, his lips brushing against her ear. "And who knows? Maybe it'll even give us some extra benefits— like in the bedroom."

Sara pulled away slightly, raising an eyebrow at him. "Really? You think steroids are going to help with that?"

Adam smirked, his confidence slowly returning. "Maybe."

Sara rolled her eyes playfully, but there was a suggestion of a smile on her lips. "Well, we'll see about that."

She looked around the bathroom one more time before stepping back and heading out. "I don't want to find you on the floor again Adam."

"You won't, I promise." Adam replied.

Once Sara was gone, Adam let out a long, shaky exhale. That sucked. The tension in his chest lingered as he glanced around at the mess he'd created. His eyes landed on the syringe lying on the floor where he had dropped it.

He picked it up, turning it over in his fingers. Holding it up to the light, he noticed the tip was smeared with his blood, a stark reminder of what he had just done. For a moment, he simply stared at it, the weight of his actions sinking in, mingling with a strange mix of pride, fear, and regret.

CHAPTER 4

The following weeks passed in a haze of workouts, injections, and an unrelenting drive that bordered on obsession. Adam was all in, fully committed to the transformation he was chasing. But even as his body began to change—subtle lines of muscle forming where there had once been none—the shadows in his life remained.

His relationship with Sara remained strained, the distance between them lingering like an unspoken truth. Even though their sex life had improved, the intimacy they once shared felt hollow, like something vital had slipped away. It should have felt like progress, but it didn't. More often than not, their moments together left him feeling empty, his mind too consumed by his own flaws to truly connect. Every encounter ended the same way—him staring at his reflection in the mirror, searching for the man he wanted to be and finding only disappointment.

At work, Adam found it harder and harder to focus. His thoughts were constantly elsewhere, consumed by the next workout, the next injection, the next step in his transformation. He sat at his desk, staring at his screen, his fingers scrolling through bodybuilding forums and articles about steroids. Each new steroid, each new method, felt like a puzzle piece he needed to complete himself.

Adam poured himself into the gym, chasing progress like it was the only thing keeping him afloat. His workouts had become something else entirely—grueling, relentless, and more intense than ever. He was lifting heavier weights than he'd ever thought possible, pushing his body to its limits with every rep and every set. The soreness in his muscles felt like validation, proof that he was finally making progress.

Chest day, Adam's favorite day was starting strong. After a few warm-up sets, he grabbed the 70-pound dumbbells, a far cry from the meager 30-pounders he had struggled with just two months ago. Sitting on the flat bench, he hoisted the heavy weights onto his knees, pausing for a steadying breath. Then, with practiced precision, he fell back onto the bench and brought the dumbbells above his chest, ready to push through his set.

As he focused on his reps, the familiar figure of the faux-hawk, gym dude loomed into view. Without so much as a word of acknowledgment, the man hovered over Adam, his impatient energy palpable.

"I need those," the gym dude said flatly. Then, without waiting, he reached out to grab the weights mid-set.

Adam's simmering frustration boiled over. He slammed the 70-pound dumbbells down with such force that the ground shook, the echo reverberating through the gym. Heads turned. Conversations stopped.

Adam shot to his feet, his face twisted in rage.

"Can't you see I'm using them, asshole!" he shouted, his voice cutting through the stunned silence. Before the gym dude could react, Adam shoved him hard. The force sent the man stumbling backward into the mirror wall with a loud thud.

For a moment, everything froze. The gym dude's mouth opened like he wanted to say something, but no words came. He backed off, his expression a mix of shock and embarrassment, before turning and walking away without another glance.

Adam stood there, breathing heavily, fists clenched at his sides. He looked around the room, taking in the wide-eyed, concerned faces staring back at him. A small, smug smile crept onto his face.

They were watching him. Not ignoring him, not mocking him. Watching.

He felt a flicker of satisfaction. He was doing it. He was changing. Finding the respect he had been chasing, the dominance he needed to feel. None of their opinions mattered—not really. They weren't part of his world. Nothing mattered except the workout, the progress, and the PUMP.

Adam could feel it every time he curled a dumbbell, every time he pressed a barbell above his chest—the burn in his muscles, the swell of his veins. It was intoxicating. But with the physical changes came something darker.

Adam's temper had become shorter. He found himself snapping at Sara over small things—whether it was something she said or something she did. He knew it wasn't fair to her, but he couldn't help it. The steroids were changing him, not just physically, but emotionally.

That night, Adam came home to find Sara sitting on the couch, scrolling through her phone. She looked up as he walked in, her eyes tired.

"Hey," she said softly. "How was the gym?"

"Fine," Adam grunted, tossing his gym bag on the floor.

Sara raised an eyebrow.

"You seem upset. Everything okay, baby?"

Adam shrugged, his body still buzzing with adrenaline still.

"I'm fine Sara."

"Adam, talk to me," Sara said, standing up and walking over to him.

"You've been so distant lately. And I don't just mean physically. You're not yourself."

Adam sighed. He could feel the frustration bubbling up inside him, the pressure building.

"I'm just focused Sara." he muttered, not meeting her eyes.

Sara frowned, reaching out to touch his arm.

"I know things have been tough, but you don't have to go through this alone. I'm here for you, you know that, right?"

Adam pulled away from her touch, his jaw clenched.

"I don't need your help, Sara. I said I'm fine, I've got this under control."

Sara blinked, clearly taken aback by his harsh tone.

"I wasn't saying you didn't. I just—"

"I said I've got it under control!" Adam snapped, his voice louder than he intended.

Sara took a step back, her expression hurt.

"Adam, please. I'm just trying to help."

For a moment, there was silence between them, the tension thick in the air. Adam could feel the anger coursing through his veins, the steroids amplifying every emotion, every reaction. He clenched and unclenched his fists.

"I don't need your help." Adam repeated, his voice cold.

Sara stared at him, her eyes glistening with unshed tears. She opened her mouth to say something, but then closed it, shaking her head. Without another word, she turned and walked toward the bedroom, leaving Adam standing there.

CHAPTER 5

The office was buzzing with its usual sounds of ringing phones and the faint droning of the old air conditioning. It was a typical day at Adam's shit job, with the mundane co-workers in their cubicles, making calls to potential buyers, pushing for that next sale. Adam sat in his small cubicle, headset on, as he ran through his list of leads, trying to close something so Mr. Louis would get off his ass. He was dressed in his usual button-down shirt, a bit crumpled from the long morning, and his face wore the expression of someone tired of routine.

George popped up from behind the cubicle wall, dressed in a good-fitting navy blue suit and grinning widely.

"Yo what's up, bro?" George asked, leaning against the cubicle wall.

Adam looked up, and his face brightened a little when he saw George. While his constant state of positivity annoyed him, George was still one of his only friends.

"George! Happy birthday, man!" Adam smiled, reaching out for a fist bump.

"Thanks, bro! Thought you forgot." George said with a smirk.

Adam chuckled. "It's tough to forget with Facebook–"

George gave a sly smile.

"Fuckin' Facebook. So–we are going out tonight... You're coming right?"

Adam hesitated for a moment.

"Tonight? I don't know, man. I've got to work out tonight. I'm trying to stick to it, you know?"

George, ever the persuasive one, rolled his eyes dramatically.

"Work out? Player look at you! Got them dick veins in the forearms now. Barely fitting in those classic Adam plaid shirts anymore either. Take a break for one day. Besides, it's my birthday!"

Adam scratched the back of his neck absentmindedly, wincing as a sharp sting shot through his skin. A pimple had burst under his nail.

"Dick veins?" he muttered to himself, glancing down at the smear of blood now on his fingertip. Grimacing, he wiped it on his pants and let out a frustrated sigh.

"Yeah dick veins, like you know when your dick is hard you get veins showing and shit? Your forearms get veiny like that so the term is dick veins."

George grabbed Adam's shoulder.

"Bro you put on some size! Very different from chips for lunch Adam. So let's celebrate that too tonight, over drinks, for my birthday."

"I don't know. I'm—"

George cut him off, flashing a mischievous grin.

"Come on, dude. Just one drink. You can bring your better half." he said.

"Coo?"

George put out his fist to confirm. Adam reluctantly fist bumped him.

George's grin widened.

"My ninja! I'll text you the details later."

He then ducked around a corner to hide from Mr. Louis and left.

As George sauntered back to his desk, Adam picked up his phone and typed out a quick message to Sara: George invited us for drinks tonight. Are you free?

A moment later, his phone buzzed with her reply: Already have plans, babe. I don't even like George. Have fun without me! Xoxo.

Adam sighed. He wasn't surprised. Sara had never really gotten along with George, and she rarely joined in on these last-minute gatherings. Still, it would've been nice to have her by his side tonight. He tossed his phone down, grabbed his headset, and refocused on his work.

Later that night, back at home, Adam sat at the kitchen table, a muscle magazine open in front of him. As he flipped through the glossy pages, he found himself drawn to the images of sculpted physiques and chiseled strength. The idea of becoming the muscular, fit version of himself he'd always envisioned felt intoxicating. It was more than just a dream—it was a sense of control in a world that often felt chaotic and unpredictable.

His phone buzzed with a text from George: Hot Spot on 17th, 8 pm. C ya bro!

Adam chuckled to himself, but then his eyes drifted down to the magazine. A sudden wave of uncertainty hit him. He was torn. On one hand, he didn't want to miss George's birthday, but on the other, he had been working so hard on his diet and workout routine. Going out meant a night of drinks, and he knew that one drink could easily turn into four or five.

Still, it was George's birthday. "Fuck it", he said to himself. He pushed the magazine aside, stood up, and headed toward the bathroom.

Adam stood in front of his bathroom mirror, staring at his reflection. He flexed slightly, inspecting his physique. He wasn't exactly where he wanted to be yet, but he was getting there. Still, the thought of missing the gym tonight weighed heavily on his mind. He needed to stay consistent, and tonight could throw off his progress.

"Okay," he muttered to himself. "Easy shot tonight, then go out and have some fun."

He reached into the bathroom drawer and pulled out a small vial of finaplix, the potent animal anabolic steroid he'd been using for nearly two months.

Adam shook the vial, watching the brownish liquid swirl inside. Popping in his fill needle, he drew out the 1 CC dose, the act so routine now it felt almost normal. Taking a deep breath, he stared at the needle and flicked out the air bubbles, his reflection in the mirror catching his eye.

"Let's get this over with," he muttered, pulling down his pants to expose his butt cheek.

His hand trembled as he positioned the needle, the tip hovering just above his skin. Slowly, he pushed it in, wincing as it sliced through muscle and past scar tissue from previous injections. The pain was sharper this time, a reminder of the damage he was doing to himself. When the full inch-long needle was buried, he pressed down on the plunger, watching the thick, brownish liquid disappear into his body.

When he finally pulled the needle out, a small bead of blood welled up at the injection site. Adam grabbed a tissue, wiping it away quickly before massaging the area, something he'd read online to help prevent lumps.

"Okay," he muttered under his breath, massaging in slow circles. "Rub it in."

But just as he started to relax, a sudden wave of dizziness hit him. His chest tightened, his vision blurred, and his knees buckled slightly. He stumbled backward, catching himself on the sink just in time to avoid collapsing.

Leaning against the counter, he gripped the edge with trembling hands, taking deep, shallow breaths. The room spun, and for a moment, he thought he might pass out. He blinked rapidly, willing the dizziness to pass. Slowly, the tightness in his chest eased, and his vision began to clear.

Straightening up, Adam stared at his reflection in the mirror. His face was pale, his eyes sunken. He ran a hand through his hair, shaking his head in disbelief.

"You look like death, man," he muttered to himself.

For a moment, he considered stopping, throwing the vial and syringe away and forgetting about all of it. But the thought was fleeting. As the dizziness faded completely, so did the fear.

He splashed water on his face, taking one last look at the mirror before turning away. He had to get ready for tonight. George was counting on him, and a night out wouldn't hurt. After all, he'd been pushing himself hard lately. One night off couldn't ruin everything, right?

The night was crisp as Adam stepped out of his apartment, dressed in a denim jacket and dark jeans. His hair was slicked back, and he was feeling slightly better after the earlier episode in the bathroom. The place George had texted him about, Hot Spot was a popular bar on 17th Street. The place was known for its rooftop views and strong cocktails—definitely a cool place for a night of drinking.

As he walked down the street, he thought about Sara. He couldn't shake her text from earlier. She'd always been critical of George, but Adam still didn't quite get why. George could be immature and reckless at times, but he was fun. He made life a little less predictable, a little less monotonous.

Adam's phone buzzed again. It was another message from George: Where you at, man? I'm already three drinks in!

Adam smiled and quickened his pace.

The bar was packed when he arrived. The rooftop glowed with soft, neon lights, and the sound of laughter and clinking glasses filled the air. George spotted him immediately and waved him over.

"Bro!" George shouted over the music, wrapping an arm around Adam's shoulders. "You made it! I was starting to think you bailed on me."

George had changed from his earlier outfit and now wore a simple white T-shirt over some jeans with a leather jacket thrown over it.

Adam grinned, though his smile was a little forced. He was still feeling off from the injection, but he didn't want to ruin the night for George.

"Wouldn't miss it, man. Happy birthday!"

George handed him a drink. "First one's on me."

Adam took the glass and raised it in a toast. "To another year, George."

They clinked glasses, and Adam downed the drink quickly. He wasn't much of a drinker these days, but tonight, he'd make an exception for George.

As the night wore on, the drinks kept flowing, and soon Adam felt looser. The alcohol dulled his earlier worries, allowing him to sink into the moment. He and George laughed over shared stories, most of them revolving around work and the absurdities they dealt with at the office. George regaled Adam with tales of his failed attempts to charm female clients, while Adam recounted the chaos of juggling his new strict workout routine with the demands of Sara.

"So, where's Sara tonight?" George asked, swirling his drink.

"She already had plans." Adam replied casually.

George raised an eyebrow.

"You need to watch that one, man."

Adam frowned.

"How so?"

"She's way out of your league, bro. Women like that?

They can't be trusted," George said with a laugh, clinking his glass against Adam's.

"Out of my league? Seriously? I think she's trustworthy. I mean, we've had our issues, but what couple doesn't?" Adam replied, his tone defensive.

George leaned back, smirking.

"Do you remember that work picnic we had a couple of months ago?"

"Yeah..." Adam said slowly, sensing something ominous.

George hesitated, his smirk fading.

"Well, when you were getting food, she was—" He suddenly stopped and waved it off.

"You know what, man? Fuck it! Tonight's a celebration. No need to ruin the mood."

Adam leaned forward, his eyes narrowing.

"No, tell me, George. You can't just bring something like that up and not finish it."

"It's nothing, man. I'm drunk." George laughed.

"You're not that drunk bro. What happened at the picnic?"

George tried to laugh it off some more, but Adam grabbed him by the jacket, pulling him closer.

"Tell me, god damn it," Adam demanded, his voice low but firm.

A few of George's friends at the table perked up, glancing their way like they were ready to step in, but George waved them off with a casual hand.

"All good," he assured them, gently removing Adam's grip.

"Fine. Buy me another shot and I'll tell you."

George said with a grin, though his eyes avoided Adam's.

The bartender placed two shots in front of them, and the men knocked them back. Adam kept his gaze locked on George, unwavering.

"Speak," Adam muttered, his tone clipped.

George sighed and leaned forward.

"Alright, chill. Let me think. Right, the picnic. So, while you walked away to grab food, she was flirting with some guy."

Adam's stomach sank.

"Who?" he asked, his voice tense.

George rubbed the back of his neck.

"I don't remember, man. And, honestly, now that I think about it–yeah, it was harmless, bro. Nothing to worry about."

Adam's eyes narrowed.

"You sure?"

George leaned back, raising his hands.

"I'm your friend, man. If it was something real, I'd be the first to kick his ass. You know that, right?"

Adam exhaled and nodded reluctantly.

"Yeah, I guess."

George slapped Adam on the shoulder.

"Good. Now let's drink and be merry, because I feel old as fuck today!"

The group around them cheered and toasted, but Adam wasn't listening. George's comment about Sara lingered in his mind like an unwanted guest, refusing to leave.

As midnight rolled around, the weight of the night started catching up to him. The drinks, the injection, the guilt of skipping his workout—all of it combined into a heavy fog that settled over his mind. Leaning against the bar, he stared down at his empty glass, feeling the room spin ever so slightly.

"You alright, man?" George asked, noticing Adam's sudden quietness.

Adam forced a small smile.

"Yeah, I'm good."

George frowned.

"You don't look it. Wanna call it a night?"

Adam nodded, grateful for the out.

"Yeah, I think I need to."

George gave him a firm pat on the back.

"No worries. Thanks for coming out, bro. Means a lot."

Adam offered a weak smile in return as they parted ways.

But as he stepped out into the cold night air, George's words played on repeat in his mind, each one chipping away at the fragile sense of control he had been clinging to.

Adam made his way down the stairs, out of the bar, and into the cool night air. The streets were quieter now, and as he walked to his car, he couldn't shake the feeling that something was off.

Maybe it was the combination of everything—the pressure of keeping up a job he hated, the drugs, the constant push to be better, stronger.

Or maybe it was just the alcohol. Either way, he knew tonight wasn't the win he thought it could be.

He arrived home, tossing his jacket onto the couch and collapsing onto the bed without even bothering to undress. His phone buzzed one last time—another text from Sara: Hope you are having fun babe. Xoxo.

Adam stared at the screen, his fingers hovering over the keyboard. He began to type:

Where the fuck are you? It's 1 a.m!

But as soon as the words appeared, he hesitated. With a frustrated sigh, he erased the message.

He wanted to be better, to rise above the insecurities that gnawed at him. He wanted to be more than the man who let anger and doubt control him. But tonight had been a harsh reminder—he still had a long way to go.

With a heavy sigh, he closed his eyes and drifted off to sleep, the sounds of the city fading into the background.

CHAPTER 6

The night was still when Adam jolted awake, his heart hammering in his chest and his forehead slick with sweat. George's voice echoed in his mind, relentless and taunting, repeating the same words.

"She was flirting with this guy. Flirting. She wants him, not you. She's out of your league, Adam."

Adam lay there, his breaths shallow and uneven, as the remnants of the dream clung to him like a shadow. He wiped a hand over his face, trying to dispel the unease twisting in his gut. Turning his head to the side, he saw Sara sleeping peacefully beside him. Her chest rose and fell in a steady rhythm, her features soft and serene in the dim light.

She looked so calm, so beautiful—so unattainable. The words George had said resurfaced, louder this time, gnawing at his already fragile confidence. Adam stared at her for a long moment, torn between the love that still anchored him to her and the doubt George had planted like a seed in his mind.

With a quiet sigh, Adam shifted onto his back, his eyes fixed on the ceiling as the silence of the night pressed down on him. Sleep refused to return. Instead, questions swirled in his head. Was George right? Was Sara really out of his league? Could she actually be hiding something from him?

Those thoughts stayed with him long after the darkness of night began to lift, lingering in the corners of his mind as morning arrived.

The kitchen was a mess—plates and bowls cluttered the countertops, and some of last night's dishes still lingered in the sink. Adam sat at the small kitchen table, tearing through his breakfast like he hadn't eaten in days. His plate was piled high with scrambled eggs and oatmeal, a testosterone-fueled meal he devoured with almost mechanical efficiency. Since starting steroids, his appetite had skyrocketed, and it showed in the way he shoveled food into his mouth, barely pausing to breathe.

Sara walked into the kitchen, her hair slightly tousled from sleep, wearing a loose shirt and pajama pants. She scanned the disarray around her before her gaze landed on Adam, who was midway through lifting another forkful of food to his mouth.

"Morning," she said, yawning as she moved to the coffee machine.

"You got home late, huh?" Adam replied, his words muffled through a mouthful of eggs.

"Not that late. Did you have fun with George?" Sara asked, pouring herself a cup of coffee. She took a sip, then joined Adam at the table, sliding into the chair across from him.

Adam wiped his mouth with the back of his hand, suddenly feeling uneasy. He cleared his throat before speaking.

"He actually said something last night about the company picnic. You remember the one from a few months ago?" Sara set her coffee cup down, her expression neutral. "Yeah, I remember. What did George say about it?"

Adam shrugged, trying to sound casual, though his heart was pounding. "Nothing really. He just kinda brought it up."

Sara tilted her head slightly, her expression still unreadable. "Sort of random, huh?"

Adam hesitated, his fork hovering over his plate. Then, deciding to push a little further, he added, "He also said you're out of my league."

Sara let out a soft laugh and leaned back in her chair, her lips curving into an amused smile.

"Did he?"

Adam nodded, watching her closely, his chest tightening. He didn't know what he expected her to say, but the question loomed in his mind: Was she really out of my league?

Sara reached across the table and took his hand, her fingers warm and gentle. She gave it a small squeeze, her expression softening.

"Adam, I think we both bring something to the table. That's why I love you." She leaned forward and pressed a kiss to his forehead, her lips warm against his skin.

Before he could respond, Sara stood up, taking her coffee with her as she walked back toward the bedroom. Adam remained at the table, his fork still in his hand, staring after her. The words she had said echoed in his mind, but they didn't quiet the doubts stirring deep inside him.

Adam stared down the hallway at the bedroom door, a strange weight pressing down on his chest. Sara's words had been comforting, but the way she'd left so quickly gnawed at him. Was she being evasive? Or was he just letting his insecurities get the better of him?

Shaking his head, he pushed the thoughts aside and finished his breakfast, his appetite now dulled. He cleared his plate, cleaning up the mess in the kitchen as best as he could before grabbing his work bag and heading for the door.

Arriving at work, Adam dropped into his cubicle chair, wincing as a sharp pain shot through his backside. He'd completely forgotten about the injection from the night before, but now it was impossible to ignore. He shifted carefully, grimacing as he tried to find a comfortable position, moving like an old man avoiding an injury.

As he adjusted in his seat, George stumbled into view, looking worse for wear. His bloodshot eyes were framed by dark circles, and he cradled his head like it might roll off his shoulders. Even his usually pristine tie hung loosely around his neck, a sight Adam had never seen before.

"Oh my God," George groaned, squinting against the fluorescent glare of the office lights. "Why did my birthday have to fall on a weekday?"

Adam chuckled. "Yeah, you went pretty hard, man."

"Hard?" George scoffed, leaning against Adam's cubicle. "I went full-on white girl at brunch, bro." He leaned in conspiratorially and whispered, "I woke up with the condom still on my dick."

Adam recoiled, his face twisting in disgust. "At least you were safe, I guess. Who even—who did you sleep with?"

George grinned like a kid caught doing something mischievous. "That girl at the bar with me. What's her name... Cindy?"

Adam nodded slowly, trying to keep up. "Cindy. Yeah."

George scratched his head, frowning slightly. "Man, I don't even remember half of what happened last night."

Adam raised an eyebrow. "Do you actually remember anything?"

George straightened up proudly. "Woke up praying to the porcelain god."

Adam frowned, confused. "Praying to the what?"

"The toilet, man! I must've been puking before I passed out."

Adam winced, shaking his head. George's ability to turn even the simplest night out into a disaster never ceased to amaze—or repulse—him.

"Didn't even have time to brush my teeth," George added with a grin, leaning in as if to share some terrible secret.

Adam pushed him back, thoroughly grossed out.

"Okay, come on, man. That's disgusting."

"Relax, dude. I'm kidding." George laughed, raising his hands in mock innocence. "I always brush my teeth—and my balls." He wagged his eyebrows suggestively. "It's a whole routine—"

Adam held up a hand, cutting him off. "Alright,

enough. I get it."

George smirked, putting his hands up like he was surrendering. "Fine, I'm done."

Adam hesitated, then decided to bring up what had been gnawing at him all morning. "You remember what you said about Sara last night? Something about the company picnic?"

George's brow furrowed, genuine confusion washing over his face. "Sara was at the picnic?"

Adam stared at him, disbelief mounting. "Yes, with me. You don't remember?"

George scratched his head again. "Man, I don't know. I was drunk. Forget I said anything alright?"

Adam sighed, waving it off. "Sure whatever."

George rubbed his temples, clearly trying to piece together the night.

"Hey has Mr. Louis seen you yet?" Adam asked, changing the subject.

"Nah," George groaned, checking his watch.

"But it's almost time for his daily tell Adam what he needs to do better routine, so I'm gonna go hide somewhere."

George started to shuffle off but paused and turned back. "Hey, thanks for coming out last night, man. I appreciate it."

Adam nodded, watching George stumble away like a wounded animal. Despite the chaos George brought with him, Adam couldn't help but appreciate the guy's loyalty.

As Adam shifted in his chair again, the sharp soreness from the injection flared, making him wince. He adjusted his position and put on his headset, forcing himself to focus on the day's calls. But no matter how hard he tried, his mind kept wandering back to Sara, George's words, and the doubts they had stirred.

The rest of the day passed in a monotonous blur—calls, emails, and the usual office grind. By the time evening came, Adam felt drained. But as he clocked out and walked to his car, a wave of relief washed over him. Work was done for the day.

Driving home, the streets were bathed in the golden hues of the setting sun. Adam's thoughts drifted from work to Sara, and back to the conversation with George. Was Sara out of his league? Was there something he was missing?

As he pulled into the driveway of his house, he took a deep breath, maybe it was time to have a real conversation with Sara—lay everything on the table and get some answers.

Adam turned off the engine and sat there for a moment, staring at the apartment complex. His mind raced with questions, but what would he do if the answer was something he didn't want to hear… What then?

CHAPTER 7

Adam stood by the sink, staring at the neatly arranged paraphernalia laid out before him. A syringe, alcohol swabs, and a small, unlabeled vial sat ominously on the counter like tools of a dark ritual.

He picked up the vial, its weight familiar in his hand. This was a routine now—one he dreaded but couldn't abandon. He knew exactly what came next: pain.

With a deep breath, Adam steadied his shaking hands and went to work. He filled the syringe with practiced precision, watching as the needle drew in the thick, golden liquid. His heart pounded against his ribs, each beat echoing his growing unease. His last injection hadn't gone smoothly; the lump it left behind on his right butt cheek was still tender, a swollen reminder of his desperation.

Glancing at the mirror, Adam studied his reflection. His body had changed over the past month, no doubt about that. His chest was broader, his arms thicker, his once-slender frame now carrying more bulk. But was it enough? Was he really getting closer to the image in his head?

"Getting there," he muttered, though the words felt hollow.

Despite the physical gains, the toll was beginning to weigh on him. His muscles might be growing, but so were the doubts clawing at his mind. Was this worth it? All this pain, the secrecy, the sacrifices? His gaze dropped to the needle in his hand.

"This is what it takes," he whispered, as if trying to convince himself.

He yanked his sweatpants down, trying to position the needle for his left cheek this time. But no matter how he twisted his body, the angle was wrong. His muscles, tight from fatigue, refused to cooperate. Frustration bubbled up, and with a groan, he abandoned the attempt and went for the sore right cheek again.

The needle pierced his swollen flesh, and Adam hissed through gritted teeth. A sharp, searing pain radiated from the injection site, but he forced himself to push the plunger. The thick liquid moved slowly, each second stretching into an eternity. Sweat beaded on his forehead and dripped down his neck as he fought the urge to scream. His legs trembled under him, but he refused to stop.

When it was finally over, Adam gasped, dropping the syringe into the sink. "Fuuuuuck," he groaned, rubbing the throbbing area in a futile attempt to ease the pain. A wave of dizziness hit him, and nausea churned in his stomach.

He looked up into the mirror, his reflection staring back at him like a stranger. His face was pale yet flushed, his eyes sunken with dark circles that made him look perpetually tired. His body was undeniably bigger, but it wasn't the image of strength and confidence he had envisioned. Instead, he saw exhaustion, doubt, and pain. Even his hairline seemed suspiciously thin, another possible casualty of his choices.

Adam shook his head, splashed cold water on his face, and forced himself to stand upright. There was no turning back now and tonight was leg day.

Adam walked into the gym, an oversized hoodie draped over his shoulders. These days, he kept himself covered, partly to avoid drawing attention and partly because, despite everything, he still felt self-conscious.

The gym buzzed with activity, a cacophony of weights clanging, treadmills whirring, and voices chatting in groups.

Adam limped toward the weight area, each step a painful reminder of the injection site still throbbing in his ass.

Ignoring the discomfort, Adam made his way to the free weights and grabbed a pair of dumbbells. He started with a warm-up set of stiff-legged deadlifts, feeling the stretch run through his hamstrings. It felt good—at least at first—but it did nothing to dull the persistent throbbing. He gritted his teeth and pushed forward. He had to. Pushing through the pain was part of the process. That's what it took. Or at least, that's what he kept telling himself.

After a brief warm-up, Adam settled onto the leg extension machine, adjusting the seat and setting the weight low to ease into his first real set.

The familiar burn in his legs was manageable—nothing compared to the sharp, lingering sting from his earlier injection. As he pushed through each rep, his mind kept circling back to the bathroom, replaying the moment on an endless loop. That shot had been brutal, but he couldn't dwell on it. He had to move past it. No pain, no gain—wasn't that the rule?

After finishing the leg extensions, he moved on to the leg press machine. His quads burned with every push, but he forced himself to keep going. One set. Two sets. By the third, his legs felt like they might give out. The muscles screamed for mercy, but stopping wasn't an option.

Next on his routine was the barbell squat- Pumping Iron had drilled its importance into his head. Adam limped toward the squat rack, wincing as the pain in his right cheek flared with every step. He loaded the bar with a pair of 45-pound plates for his warm-up set. Standing back, he smirked to himself. Not too long ago, this had been his max. Sliding under the bar, he adjusted it on his shoulders, positioned his feet, and braced himself. Down he went. One. Up. Two. Up. But as he sank into the third squat, his legs began to wobble beneath him.

The pain radiating from the injection site surged down through his thighs, hot and unrelenting. His body faltered, and he stumbled as he racked the bar, narrowly avoiding disaster. He stood there for a moment, clutching the bar for support, his chest heaving. He tried to shake it off, to reset, but his body was done for the night.

Frustrated, Adam limped toward the exit, each step a painful reminder of his limits. He cursed under his breath, the words bitter on his tongue. Strength and progress felt further away than ever, and the weight of failure pressed down harder than any barbell ever could.

The next morning, sunlight streamed through the curtains of Adam's bedroom, illuminating the room in a soft glow. He lay sprawled on the bed, drenched in sweat, his body radiating heat like a furnace. His head throbbed with a dull, relentless ache, and every muscle felt like it had been pummeled into submission.

The alarm blared on the nightstand, its shrill tone cutting through the fog in his mind. Adam groaned, barely managing to lift a clammy hand to silence it.

Next to him, Sara stirred, blinking herself awake. She rolled over, her nose wrinkling as she realized the sheets beneath him were soaked.

"Ugh, babe, you're all sweaty," she muttered, shifting away from the damp spot.

His skin felt sticky, and he could sense the feverish heat radiating off his body like a warning sign.

Sara sat up, her expression shifting to concern as she took a closer look at him.

"Adam, are you okay? You look really sick."

He swung his legs over the side of the bed and forced himself to stand, ignoring the way his body screamed in protest.

"I'm fine," he muttered, brushing her off as he stumbled toward the bathroom. He didn't want to deal with her worry, her questions, or the way her concern made him feel even weaker.

Inside the bathroom, Adam closed the door and leaned heavily against the sink, staring at his reflection in the mirror. What he saw made his stomach churn. His face was pale, almost gray, and his bloodshot eyes looked like they belonged to a man who hadn't slept in days. Sweat beaded on his forehead and clung to his skin, making him look as sick as he felt.

"What the hell is wrong with me?" he whispered, his voice cracking.

The words hung in the air as he splashed cold water onto his face, the chill briefly shocking his overheated skin. But it wasn't enough to shake the feeling that something deeper was unraveling inside him.

Dragging himself into work, Adam barely made it to his cubicle. Every step felt like a marathon, and the fluorescent lights overhead only made his headache worse. He could still feel the fever pulsing through his body, but he had a job to do.

As he passed by George's cubicle, he overheard something that made him pause.

"Okay, now I want you to put your leg above your head and—" George's voice was unmistakably loud, and Adam caught the tail end of the conversation.

George saw him out of the corner of his eye and quickly adjusted his tone.

"And—Adam! Hey, man!" he called out. Then, into the phone, he said, "Gotta go."

Adam raised an eyebrow but kept walking. "I'm not even going to ask," he muttered as he passed.

George grinned, looking like he'd just gotten away with something.

"What, that? Pfff, that was nothing. Just a weekly customer who always orders something special."

Adam gave him a blank stare. "I don't care, man. But Louis might."

As Adam tried to walk away, George jumped up and blocked his path. He gave Adam a once-over, his expression shifting from mischievous to concerned.

"Shit, bro, you look like... well, shit."

"I'm fuckin' fine George, but thanks," Adam grunted, walking away.

But the truth was, he wasn't fine. He felt like he was

falling apart, and his body was betraying him at every turn.

"Mr. Stenson!" Mr. Louis barked, his sharp eyes narrowing on Adam. "What are you doing coming to work looking like that?"

Mr. Louis recoiled in disgust, covering his mouth with his hand as if Adam were contagious.

"If you get me sick, I will kill you, then fire you."

George opened his mouth to defend Adam. "Sir, you can't—"

"Shut it, Mr. Perry," Mr. Louis snapped, cutting George off mid-sentence.

Adam tried to protest, but Mr. Louis wasn't having it. "Go home, Mr. Stenson. Get better," he ordered, pointing toward the door. There was no room for argument.

Adam sighed, his body sagging with defeat. Without another word, he turned and headed back the way he came, for once grateful for Mr. Louis.

As Adam reached the exit, George leaned over toward Mr. Louis with a sly grin.

"You know, I think I'm feeling a little sick today too. Do you—"

Mr. Louis, his expression flat and unimpressed, cut him off mid-sentence.

"Yeah? I'm feeling a little sick too. SICK OF YOUR SHIT, GEORGE!" His voice thundered through the office, turning heads. Then, just as quickly, he dropped to a calm, almost whispering tone. "Now, for Christ's sake, Mr. Perry, please go back to work."

A few curious faces peeked over the tops of cubicles, watching as George, thoroughly defeated, slumped back into his chair.

Mr. Louis smirked faintly to himself, the hint of satisfaction clear on his face, before turning and striding back to his office, leaving the rest of the room in awkward silence.

Back home, Adam stood in the bathroom once again, staring into the mirror. It's always this fucking mirror he thought. These fucking yellow light bulbs. He hated them. He hated a lot of things lately. But especially the way he felt right now. He looked worse than ever. His entire body ached, and the fever hadn't let up.

Lined up before him were the vials of steroids, their amber glass catching the light, and beside them, the needles—clean, sharp, waiting. He stared at them, his chest tightening, his pulse heavy in his ears. For a moment, doubt flickered, but it was drowned out by something stronger. He exhaled, closing his eyes briefly before opening them again, his focus sharpening.

He reached for the syringe. It was time. With trembling hands, he pulled down his pants and inspected the swollen lump on his right butt cheek. The skin was red, inflamed, and stretched taut. It looked worse than ever—angry and unforgiving.

A wave of nausea rolled through him, and Adam shook his head, gripping the edge of the sink to steady himself. He wasn't sure how much more of this he could take.

"Think I'll skip the shot today," he thought, his voice barely more than a whisper as he shoved the vial aside. He needed a break—from the needles, the expectations, and the endless cycle of pain.

CHAPTER 8

Adam felt like a stranger in his own skin as he walked through the doors of the gym, sweat already pooling under his hoodie. His body was heavy, like dragging a thousand-pound weight on his back, and each step sent a reminder of the fever and pain lingering in his body.

The gym was bright and buzzing like usual for this time of night, full of people running on treadmills, lifting weights, and chatting by the mirrors. All of them looked healthy, strong, and focused. He envied them for feeling the exact opposite of how he felt.

But Adam didn't have time to think about that. He had to work out. It was his routine. Steroids or not, the grind didn't stop, even when his body screamed for rest. He headed straight for the weights and set up for deadlifts.

The first set was light, about 135 pounds. Normally, this would be easy for him, a warm-up at best. But today, his muscles groaned in protest with each pull.

His head spun as he gripped the bar, but he still managed to get a couple of lifts in, each one slower than the last. By the time he dropped the bar, his legs wobbled underneath him. His breath came out in short, sharp bursts. The sweat poured down his face, soaking through the towel he had draped over his head.

Adam wiped his brow and added more weight, going for 225 pounds now. His arms were shaking, and his vision was starting to blur. He didn't care. He couldn't care. "Gotta get stronger," he told himself. "Gotta keep going."

He bent down to grab the bar again. The metal felt cold and heavy in his hands.

With all the strength he had left, Adam pulled. The bar barely moved. His legs strained, his back screamed, but he kept pulling. Inch by inch, he forced the weight up until it was locked in place above his knees.

His body screamed at him to stop, but he held on for a second longer before dropping the bar to the ground. The clang echoed in his ears.

For a moment, he stood there, breathless, swaying on his feet. Then, without warning, the world tilted.

Adam stumbled backward, his legs giving out beneath him. He crashed into the rack of dumbbells behind him, sending weights clattering to the floor as his body slumped over like a ragdoll. Everything went dark.

Faint voices surrounded him. Flashes of light. Pressure in his chest. Adam was dimly aware of people talking around him, but their words were muffled, like he was underwater.

A light flashed in his eyes. His vision was hazy, but he could make out a figure leaning over him. Someone was talking, their voice clear and calm.

"He's got a concussion and a high fever," the voice said, fading in and out of his consciousness. "Let's get a line going."

Adam tried to open his eyes fully, but the effort felt like trying to lift a mountain. His body was heavy, so heavy.

"He's burning up," another voice chimed in.

The sound of an ambulance siren pierced through the haze. Adam could feel the stretcher beneath him as they lifted him into the back of the vehicle. His body jolted with every bump in the road, his head throbbing with each pulse of pain.

"Driver, let's hurry!" someone called out.

The sirens screamed louder as they picked up speed.

Adam drifted in and out of consciousness, feeling the heat of his fever gnawing at him from the inside.

Somewhere in the back of his mind, he knew this was bad, worse than anything he'd ever felt before. But he couldn't muster the energy to care. Everything was fading and it felt so good to finally let it all go...

The constant beeping of a heart monitor was the first thing Adam heard when he came to. His eyes fluttered open, and he squinted against the harsh fluorescent lights overhead. His head was pounding, and his body felt stiff, like he had been lying in the same position for days.

He tried to sit up, but a sharp pain shot through his lower back, forcing him to slump back down on the pillow. Groaning, he lifted his hand to his head, rubbing his temples as he tried to remember what had happened.

"Adam?"

The voice pulled him back to reality. His vision slowly cleared, and he saw three familiar faces standing around his hospital bed—his parents and Sara. They all looked pale and worried, their eyes full of concern.

"What—where am I?" Adam croaked, his throat dry and scratchy.

He tried to prop himself up on his elbows but winced again from the pain that flared in his lower back and gave up trying to sit up.

His dad stepped forward.

"Son, you're in the hospital. You fell pretty hard at the gym. Fainted actually."

Adam blinked, confused. The gym? He asked himself. Then the memory came rushing back—the deadlift, the fall, the feeling of his body collapsing beneath him.

"Jesus," Adam muttered, rubbing his hand over his face. He still felt hot, feverish, and his whole body ached. He had no idea how long he'd been out.

"I'm just glad my boy is okay," his mom said, her voice shaky as she brushed a tear away.

Sara, who had been standing silently by the foot of the bed, stepped forward. "Glad you're okay, Adam," she whispered, her voice tight.

Before Adam could respond, the door to his hospital room swung open, and a doctor entered, clipboard in hand. He was older, with graying hair and the air of someone who had seen this scenario far too many times.

"Okay, Mr. Stenson," the doctor said, flipping through Adam's chart.

Adam's dad quickly stepped forward, "Yes?"

The doctor looked up, giving him a polite smile.

"No sir, I meant your son."

Adam raised his hand weakly. "Doc, am I gonna be okay?"

The doctor sighed, looking at Adam seriously.

"Yes, Adam, you'll be okay. You hit your head pretty hard when you collapsed, and you've been running a dangerously high fever. But that fever—" the doctor paused, his tone turning more grave, "—was caused by an infection in your right gluteus minor. That's your butt cheek."

Adam blinked. "You mean that bruise?"

The doctor shook his head and adjusted the stethoscope hanging on his neck. "That wasn't a bruise, Adam. That was an abscess, a serious infection. If it had gotten any worse, it could have been fatal. Abscesses like this usually happen because of an injection, especially when a needle is unclean."

Adam felt a cold chill crawl up his spine. His parents both stared at him, their expressions a mix of confusion and shock.

"Injection?" Mr. Stenson repeated, his voice tinged with disbelief.

"Adam, what's he talking about? What the hell are you injecting?"

Adam swallowed hard, avoiding eye contact with his dad.

"Uhm, just B12 shots. For energy," he lied, his voice

barely above a whisper.

"That's a thing?" Mr. Stenson looked over at his wife.

The doctor chimed in, "It is actually." Then gave Adam a pointed look, then glanced at Sara, who was standing awkwardly at the side of the room. She had been silent throughout the whole conversation, her eyes fixed on the floor.

The doctor sighed. "Can I speak with Adam alone, please?"

Adam's parents exchanged a glance before nodding. His dad patted Adam on the arm, and his mom gave him a gentle kiss on the forehead.

"We'll be right outside, honey," she said softly.

Once they left, the doctor turned back to Adam, his expression serious.

"Adam, it's from steroids. Your partner told me you were taking them."

Adam's heart sank. He shot a look at Sara, but she wouldn't meet his eyes.

The doctor continued, his tone steady but firm.

"Let me explain what just happened to you. Maybe it'll make you think twice about using them again."

Adam's head was reeling as the doctor explained everything. The abscess, the infection, the surgery that saved his life.

"We had to make an incision across the infected area," the doctor said, his voice calm but direct. "The infection had spread deep into your muscle, and we had to remove a lot of it. The tissue was torn and damaged. You're lucky we caught it when we did."

Adam felt a wave of nausea wash over him as the doctor continued. He could picture it all in his mind—his skin splitting open like butter, the infection oozing out, his muscle torn apart.

"When we removed the infection, we had to clean the entire area and stitch you back up," the doctor explained. "It's going to take quite some time for your body to heal from this. You may never grow muscle there again and the scar tissue–that'll never fully go away."

Adam stared at the ceiling, his throat tight. How did it come to this? He'd thought the steroids would make him stronger, tougher. But all they had done was break him down.

The doctor finished his explanation and gave Adam a long, hard look. "Steroids can kill you, Adam, and these ones almost did," he said quietly.

"They can mess with your mind, your body. They aren't worth it. You have a family that cares about you, a fiancé, right? Who loves you. They would be devastated if something happened to you."

Adam's chest tightened as he looked down at his hands, guilt settling heavy in his stomach. The doctor was right. He had been playing with fire, and he'd almost paid the price.

"Now," the doctor continued, his voice softening, "I don't want to see you back here except for regular check-ups. Okay? Take care of yourself, Mr. Stenson."

The doctor gave him a small nod before leaving the room, shaking hands with Sara and his parents who were waiting outside.

A nurse came in moments later to check his vitals.

"Adam, it's time for your family to leave. You need rest. They can pick you up in the morning."

Adam's parents and Sara came back into the room, their faces still full of concern. His dad gave him a firm pat on the shoulder.

"Son, I'm glad you're okay. Call us when you get home."

His mom leaned in, kissing his forehead again.

"I love you, Adam. Please take care of yourself."

Sara was the last to speak, her voice soft and full of emotion.

"I'll pick you up in the morning, okay? Get some rest."

Adam nodded, barely able to speak.

As they left, the reality of everything that had happened hit him all at once. He could have died because of some fucking steroids. Because he couldn't accept his limits and learn to be comfortable in his own skin.

Adam let out a frustrated sigh and slammed his head back against the pillow. His body ached, his mind felt scattered, and he felt utterly lost.

Trying to sleep away the feelings he closed his eyes and let the weight of his choices sink in. He had a long road to recovery ahead, both physically and mentally. And he knew it wouldn't be an easy fix.

His parents weren't stupid and Sara was afraid of him. All of the stupid risks he took, the substances he shot up into his body, all for nothing. He felt like a fool. He had let down those who cared about him and he had let down himself.

He ignored the obvious signs and words of warning from George and Sara and now he is literally missing a chunk of his ass. All for nothing.

Adam knew he couldn't hide behind his frustrations anymore. He couldn't blame his reality on the way people treated or perceived him anymore. This time, he couldn't hide from the truth.

CHAPTER 9

Adam's entire body screamed with pain as Sara helped him to the bed. Each step felt like a lightning bolt ripping through his body and his muscles protested with every movement. It wasn't just the physical pain from his recent hospital visit—it was the emotional toll that weighed him down. The realization of how far he had fallen hit him hard, and the look of concern permanently etched on Sara's face only deepened the pit of guilt in his stomach.

On the ride home, she stole judgmental glances nearly every second until it drove Adam mad.

"Would you stop looking at me like that? I'm not going to drop dead in the car," Adam finally said with a gruff.

"Oh that makes me feel so much better Adam! I hope you don't plan on doing any of that shit anymore!" Sara shouted at him.

"Doing what?" Adam said testily.

"You want me to spell it out for you? The fuckin' steroids Adam! I mean look at what they did to you." Sara turned to glare at Adam with wide, angry eyes.

"Just stop it, Sara. Let me get home first at least." Adam groaned, still very much in pain.

"I hope things are going to be different— for your sake."

"Wake me up when we get home and we'll talk." Adam barked.

He drifted off to restless sleep right after and only woke up when she had to get him out of the car and into their home.

Once settled in bed, Sara hovered for a moment, watching him. Her arms were crossed over her chest as if she were trying to decide what to do next. She glanced toward the bathroom, her mind clearly elsewhere, before the sound of her phone ringing snapped her attention back to reality. She grabbed it from the bedside table and answered.

"Oh, hi Mr. Stenson," Sara said quietly, her voice soothing but tired.

She ran a hand through her rich curls of hair as she spoke into the phone.

"Yeah, we just got home. He's sleeping. Of course Bob. I'll keep an eye on him. Okay, I definitely will. Bye."

Sara ended the call and walked out of the room, typing away at her phone. Before long she was on another call but chose to take this one away from Adam.

Adam opened an eye as she walked away, he was slowly waking up and trying to push back the fog of sleep that had settled over him. He felt drained, his mind was sluggish and his body was incapable of keeping up but his waking thoughts went to the phone call.

His paranoia gnawed at him till the last of the sleep escaped him. He shifted uncomfortably in bed, his side throbbing from the wound that had landed him in the hospital. He could hear Sara moving around in the kitchen, her voice muffled as she spoke on the phone. He couldn't make out the words, but the sound of her laughter carried into the room, further fueling his suspicions.

The idea that Sara might be talking to someone else, confiding in someone behind his back, felt like a knife twisting in his chest. It hurt more than the missing chunk of his ass. He had always trusted her, but the drugs had messed with his mind, making him see threats where there were none. He knew that, but knowing didn't make it any easier to dismiss the irrational and painful thoughts.

Adam's breathing grew heavier, and despite the pain, he pushed himself out of bed, stumbling as his legs wobbled beneath him. His vision swam for a moment, but he steadied himself, determined to confront Sara, to get some answers. He walked into the kitchen, still half out of it from the pain medication, and found Sara leaning against the counter with her phone in hand. She was laughing, a lightness in her voice that had been missing for weeks.

"Stop it. You know that's not funny. No, I guess I still do. I just don't want to lie—"

When Sara saw Adam, her face paled, and she quickly hung up the phone.

"How are you feeling, babe?" she asked quickly.

"Who were you talking to?" Adam asked, his voice rough and unsteady with pain and suspicion.

Sara blinked, momentarily taken aback.

"No one," she said quickly. "Just a friend checking in to see how you were doing."

Adam narrowed his eyes, feeling a wave of dizziness wash over him. He wasn't sure if it was the meds or his growing paranoia, but he didn't believe her.

"Heard from my parents?" he asked, trying to divert the conversation for a moment.

Before Sara could answer, Adam felt his knees buckle, and he slipped, falling hard onto the floor. A sharp pain shot through his side, and he cursed loudly, gripping his wound as Sara rushed over to help him.

"Fuck!" he screamed in pain.

"Adam!" she cried, her voice filled with panic. She knelt beside him, struggling to help him to his feet.

"Baby, are you okay? Here, let me help you."

Adam groaned in excruciating pain as Sara pulled him up, guiding him back to the bed. His body felt limp, helpless, and he hated it. He hated the fact that he was so dependent on her right now, that he couldn't even stand on his own without her support.

"I'm pathetic," Adam mumbled as they made their

way back to the room, his voice heavy with defeat.

"You're never too weak for the people who love you," Sara said softly, her words deliberate and steady.

Once he was back in bed, Sara stood over him, her hands on her hips.

"You just need to take it easy," she said, her voice firm. "You can't keep pushing yourself like this."

Adam's head lolled to the side, his eyelids growing heavy again. The meds were dragging him back into unconsciousness, but before he could drift off, a thought forced its way to the surface. He blinked up at Sara, his voice barely audible as he muttered,

"Sara, please don't cheat on me."

Sara froze, her heart skipping a beat. The words hung in the air like a heavy cloud, thick with accusation and doubt.

"What?" she asked, her voice barely a whisper.

"I would never–" she stammered, her mind racing to understand where this sudden insecurity was coming from. She reached out, gently feeling his forehead, checking for a fever. He was hot to the touch, but it wasn't just the medication. Something deeper was eating away at him.

"Hey I would never cheat on you," she said again, quietly this time. She leaned down and kissed Adam on his cheek softly, hoping to reassure him.

"We'll talk when you're feeling better, okay?"

Adam didn't respond. His eyes were already closed, his breathing steady as sleep finally claimed him.

She wanted to believe that things would return to normal now that he was off the drugs, but a gnawing fear lingered in the back of her mind. What if this wasn't the end but the start of something far more complicated?

Adam woke hours later, groggy but more coherent than before. The sharp pain had dulled to a persistent ache, still uncomfortable but bearable. From the kitchen, he could hear the soft hum of the coffee maker and the familiar clinking of mugs as Sara prepared breakfast.

He sat up slowly, wincing as his side throbbed in protest, and swung his legs over the edge of the bed. The weight of the previous night pressed down on him, but he knew he couldn't ignore it. He needed to talk to her, to explain himself, to try and rebuild the fragile connection between them. He couldn't let his fears and paranoia drive an even deeper wedge into their relationship.

When he walked into the kitchen, Sara was standing at the counter, pouring coffee into her mug. She glanced up when she saw him, offering him a small smile.

"What are you doing up, sleepy head? It's 7:00 am," she said, her voice soft.

"I didn't want to miss coffee with you," Adam replied, his voice still hoarse.

She smiled to herself as she poured him some coffee.

He slowly approached the counter, his steps heavy with the weight of sleeplessness. Reaching for the second mug Sara had poured, he cradled it in his hands. The heat radiating from the ceramic pressed into his palms, grounding him—reminding him he could feel something besides doubt, insecurity, and pain, if only for a moment.

Bringing the mug shakily to his lips, the rich aroma of coffee enveloped him, sharp and comforting. He took a cautious sip. The warmth spread through him, the liquid trailing heat down his throat, igniting a subtle strength within. It soothed his frayed nerves, chased away the lingering grogginess, and gave him a fragile sense of clarity.

"I—I'm sorry about last night, for accusing you," he said after a long pause.

"I don't know what came over me. I shouldn't have said what I did."

Sara set her mug down and leaned against the counter, crossing her arms.

"Do you really think I'd cheat on you?"

Adam swallowed hard, feeling the weight of her question pressing down on him.

"I don't know," he admitted. "It's just everything's been so messed up lately. I've been feeling like I'm losing control of everything—my body, my mind, our relationship. And when I heard you laughing on the phone, I guess I just let my insecurities get the best of me."

Sara's expression softened, and she stepped closer, reaching out to take his hand.

"Adam, I'm not going anywhere. I know things have been hard, but I'm here. I've always been here. You don't have to go through this alone."

Adam squeezed her hand, feeling a surge of relief.

"I'm sorry. I've been so caught up in my own head that I didn't realize how much I've been hurting you."

Sara shook her head. "We'll get through this. But you have to promise me something."

"Anything," Adam said, his voice earnest.

"No more doubting me. I am here because I love you, no more doubting that."

Adam nodded, "I promise. No more doubting," he said firmly.

CHAPTER 10

Morning light streamed through the blinds of Adam's bedroom, casting soft shadows on the walls. He stirred under the covers, his mind still foggy from pain and medication.

The events of the past few days played in his mind like a broken reel—the painful shot, the hospital, the mistrust of Sara, and the unbearable realization that his body was no longer his fortress. He reached for his phone on the nightstand, noticing the screen lit up with a notification: 10 missed calls.

Groaning, he opened his voicemail and listened.

"Hey Adam, it's your mom. Just making sure you got home safe and Sara's taking care of you. We love you very much, and if you need anything, let us know. Love you."

The warmth in his mother's voice cut through him. He hadn't called her back. What would he even say? He lied to her face and said the injections were for vitamin supplements and he knew she didn't believe him.

He deleted it.

The second message was from George.

"Player! How are you, man? I talked to Sara last night. She said you were still out of it. Holla at me if you need anything. Peace."

George's voice grated against his nerves. Why was

Sara talking to George? He shook his head, dismissing the thought.

Deleted.

The third message was from Mr. Louis who sounded as indifferent as always.

"Hey Stenson. I heard you were in the hospital. Err... get better, I guess. If it's a disease you passed to us here at work, I will gut you like a fish. If not, you've got four medical leave days left, so use them wisely."

Adam deleted it halfway through.

He tossed his phone down and sat up, bracing himself for the slow and painful process of getting to his feet. A sharp wave of discomfort shot through his body as he finally stood, his movements stiff and deliberate. Hobbling toward the bathroom, each step was a reminder of how far he'd pushed himself.

Adam reached the bathroom, his hand gripping the sink for support as he steadied himself. He looked up at the mirror, and the reflection staring back felt like a stranger. His face was pale and drawn, his arms, which once carried the bulk he'd worked so hard for, looked thinner, almost frail. The faint outline of veins that used to make him proud now seemed to mock him. It was as if all his gains had vanished in the span of a week, melting away under the weight of his own decisions. He pulled at the hem of his shirt, exposing his torso, and felt a pang of frustration. His chest looked smaller, his shoulders less defined. Everything he'd sacrificed, every painful injection and grueling workout, felt like it had been for nothing. He clenched the edge of the counter, his jaw tightening as a mix of anger and despair settled in. How had it all unraveled so quickly?

He opened the cabinet under the sink, expecting to see the familiar stash of vials and syringes neatly tucked away. But the compartment was empty. Adam froze, staring at the vacant space in disbelief. His initial confusion quickly morphed into panic. Where was his gear?!

His hands moved frantically, yanking open every drawer and rummaging through bottles and containers. The clattering echoed in the small bathroom, each empty space fueling his growing desperation. His mind raced, looping through the same thought: he needed his steroids, his syringes, his tools—anything to feel strong again. Every second without them felt like he was losing more of himself.

The days spent in the hospital had already stolen so much from him. He could feel the strength slipping away, the muscle he'd fought so hard to build fading into memory. He needed his shot to stop the backslide. He needed to fix this.

And then it hit him. Sara.

Adam froze mid-motion, his hands gripping the edge of the sink as his heart pounded. She must have taken it. His mind reeled, torn between anger and betrayal. Why would she do this? How could she? The thought sent a fresh wave of frustration coursing through him. She didn't understand—she couldn't. This wasn't just about muscle; it was about control, power, and the only thing that had made him feel like he mattered.

He clenched his fists until his nails dug into his palms.

"Where did you put it, Sara?" he muttered under his breath, his voice low and tense. The question lingered in the air as he stormed out of the bathroom, intent on finding her and demanding answers.

He grabbed his phone, and dialed her. Sara picked on the first ring with obvious excitement in her voice.

"Hey, sleepy head!"

"Where's my stuff?!" Adam replied immediately, cutting her off.

"What stuff?"

"My steroids! My fina bottles! My needles—everything, Sara! Where are they?"

Adam shouted into his phone, his voice cracking with panic. His hands trembled as he paced the room, his eyes wild and bloodshot. He looked unhinged, teetering on the edge of desperation, the words spilling out like a flood he couldn't control.

Sara's voice went quiet for a moment, and then came back, calm but firm.

"I threw it all out."

Adam's heart pounded in his chest, his muscles tensing with a mix of fury and disbelief.

"You did what?!"

"Have you forgotten what the doctor told you, Adam? For fuck's sake, that stuff isn't good for you! You know what? I'm at work! We'll talk about this when I get home!"

The line went dead before he could find something to say.

Adam stood perfectly still in the middle of the apartment, his chest heaving and his hands shaking with rage. How could she do this? How could she betray him in such a manner? He slammed his phone onto the bed, the weight of it not enough to release the anger building inside him.

With a roar, he grabbed a nearby bottle and hurled it against the wall. White hot pain shot through his side immediately, reminding him of his injury. Adam collapsed onto the bed, desperately gasping for breath.

His body was weak, and now he had no way to fix it. The painkillers on the nightstand beckoned loudly and Adam succumbed. He grabbed them and popped a few without water, desperate for any kind of relief.

He lay back down and shut his eyes tight, trying to block out the thoughts dancing around his head till eventually the world around him faded to black as the meds took hold.

When Adam finally stirred again, the room was dim, and the soft sounds of the TV played in the background. He sat up unsteadily and went to stand in front of the mirror. He took off his shirt and flexed his arms. Maybe it was just a dream? He thought.

But it wasn't a dream, the reflection that stared back at him was a shadow of his former self. His gear was gone and so were his gains. He was looking at a stranger in every sense of the word. His once strong, more defined muscles were nowhere to be found in the reflection of this loser.

The sound of Sara's keys jingled in the hallway, and moments later, she walked into the apartment. Her footsteps were light and hesitant, but the tension between them was thick as she entered the bedroom.

Adam turned to face her, his heart racing. The anger he had felt earlier bubbled back up to the surface, and he turned abruptly from the mirror, his bulging fists clenched.

"Adam, Is everything okay?"

Before she could react, Adam charged at her, his hands wrapping around her throat in a vice-like grip. He picked her up and slammed her against the wall, his eyes ablaze with fury.

"Look at me! I'm weak and pathetic! Is this what you want? And you threw away my fuckin' steroids! You!" He yelled incoherently.

Sara's eyes went instantly wide with fear as she clawed at his hands, gasping for breath.

"Adam, I can't—breathe—"

Her face began to turn red as Adam continued to cut off her air supply.

For a brief, terrifying moment, Adam considered squeezing harder and Sara thought he would have done it.

"I could fucking kill you right now!"

He could feel the power in his hands, the control he had over her life. He didn't feel weak at the moment, he didn't feel small.

But something inside him broke. His grip loosened, and he stepped back, horrified by what he had almost done.

Sara collapsed to the floor, coughing, wheezing, and gasping for air. The tears silently streamed down her face.

Adam stood frozen, his hands shaking as guilt and shame washed over him. He felt the shame swell up in him till it burst into a wave of tears and he dropped to his knees, sobbing uncontrollably.

"I'm sorry. I'm so fucking sorry, Sara!" He cried.

Sara clutched her neck, struggling to regain her composure. Staring at this pathetic man of hers weeping after almost killing her. She slowly got up and turned away to make her way out of the room when Adam grabbed her ankle, still weeping and sobbing.

"Please Sara. Please don't leave me. I'll never do that again, I don't know what I'm going to do without you."

Sara stopped in her tracks and looked down at the begging Adam, her face a mix of fear and sadness.

"If you ever touch me like that, you'll never see me again."

Adam nodded, his body trembling. He had lost control, and the person he saw in the mirror—the person capable of hurting the woman he loved—was someone he didn't recognize.

"I don't know what's happening to me, Sara."

He sank back to the floor, his chest heaving as he struggled to breathe. The panic attack came suddenly as panic gripped him, and soon, his breathing became erratic. His mind was more than happy to spin out of control.

Sara, despite everything, knelt beside him, placing a hand on his shoulder.

"Breathe, Adam. Breathe."

Her voice was steady, her touch gentle as she guided him through slow, deep breaths.

It took a while, but eventually, Adam's breathing slowed, and the panic began to subside. He sat there, his body weak and trembling, as Sara sat next to him, her hand still on his shoulder.

They stayed like that for a long time, neither saying a word. Sara held Adam tightly, and he clung to her as if she were the only thing keeping him from sinking completely. In that moment, they were both raw and fragile, two broken pieces trying to hold each other together as the light outside faded and the day quietly slipped away.

CHAPTER 11

Adam stood in the middle of the living room, arms crossed, watching Sara sift through the mess he'd been too overwhelmed to tackle on his own. The room looked like his mind: cluttered and unsure, unsure of what should stay and what should go. She held up a stack of his old bodybuilding magazines.

"Adam, what should I do with these?" she asked, shaking the magazines slightly as if to wake him from his daze.

He shrugged. "Toss them," he said flatly, avoiding eye contact.

"You sure?" She looked at him carefully, knowing full well how hard this was for him.

Adam's jaw tightened. "Yeah, I'm done with that."

Sara nodded and tossed the magazines into the trash without a word. The soft thud of glossy pages hitting the bottom of the bin carried a strange sense of finality, one that made Adam's stomach twist.

Nobody collected magazines anymore, but holding them in his hands had made everything feel real. The photos of professionals on paper had connected him to his dream in a way nothing else did. Now, watching them disappear, he wasn't sure if he was truly ready to let go.

She stepped closer, gently brushing her fingers against his arm.

"Babe," she said softly, "I think today's the day we take the bandage off for good."

Adam tensed, his heart speeding up.

"I don't think I'm ready–"

Sara gave him a small, encouraging smile.

"I'll help you. You don't have to do it alone."

He swallowed, hesitating. He hadn't looked at it since the surgery, he tried not to remember it at all. The idea of seeing the scar, that jagged mark running up his ass cheek, made him feel queasy. The accident at the gym had been humiliating enough—passing out in front of everyone—but now there was this ugly reminder of it stuck to his body forever.

"I don't know if I can watch it," Adam admitted, his voice quieter than he meant for it to be.

Sara reached for his hand, giving it a gentle squeeze.

"You don't have to."

Together, they walked into the bathroom. The harsh yellow bathroom lights reflected off the pristine surfaces, everything sterile and needle-free now. He didn't look at the mirror. He knew that wasn't a good idea.

Sara sat down on the toilet, bringing herself to eye level with the bandage. Adam's fingers trembled as he tugged at the waistband of his sweatpants, slowly revealing the bandage stuck to his side.

Sara moved with careful precision, her fingers peeling back the tape that had held the bandage in place for over a week now. Adam winced as the adhesive pulled at his skin, but he bit back the discomfort. He felt exposed, vulnerable.

"Ready?" Sara asked, her voice gentle.

"No." Adam replied jokingly.

Sara smirked and with a final tug, the bandage came off. Sara's eyes lingered on the scar for a moment before she spoke.

"It's healed, but it's pretty gnarly looking," she said softly.

Adam didn't want to look, but his curiosity got the

better of him. His stomach twisted when he saw it—an angry, jagged line running up his ass cheek like a cruel reminder of his weakness. He clamped a hand over his mouth, nausea rising.

"It'll fade," Sara said quickly, standing up to face him. "The doctor said you can go back to the gym once it's healed. At least you can start lifting again."

But Adam shook his head.

"It's weird knowing a lot of people saw me pass out there."

Sara stepped closer and kissed him, her lips soft and warm against his cheek.

"No one knows you there," she whispered. "You'll be fine."

But Adam knew that they knew him there.

Later that night, Adam found himself outside the gym. It was his first time back since the accident. His hoodie was pulled low over his face, gym bag in hand as he slowly made his way through the parking lot.

Every part of him screamed to turn around, to run, but something kept him rooted to the spot.

Before he could decide what to do, a familiar voice cut through the evening air.

"Yo, Adam right?!"

Adam's heart sank. It was Jason, the bodybuilder who had spotted him when he first began lifting. Jason was still the biggest guy he had ever seen, the kind of guy who looked like he could bench press a car without breaking a sweat.

"Hey–what's up," Adam muttered, keeping his eyes down, trying to walk past him.

Jason wasn't having it.

"Hey, slow down for a second," he said, his voice calm but commanding.

Reluctantly, Adam stopped and looked over at Jason

who was walking towards him now. He could feel his pulse pounding in his ears, nervous sweat breaking out on his forehead.

As Jason got close he extended a hand.

"Jason."

"I know who you are," he replied, shaking it, feeling like a child in comparison to the giant standing in front of him. Jason didn't waste any time.

"I saw you pass out that night," he said, a grin forming at the corner of his mouth. "You good?"

Adam nodded, "Yeah all good now." Lying through his teeth.

"Glad you good bro. Man, you were going hard, bro. Almost as hard as me. You made some gains too."

"Not enough," Adam quickly mumbled.

"I feel that." Jason laughed.

"You do?" Adam asked, his voice quiet, unsure.

Jason leaned in slightly, lowering his voice.

"I had that problem too. It affected my life because I wasn't growing. Confidence was down, sex rarely happened, almost a thing of the past at one point. That shit all changed the moment I jumped on a proper cycle."

"A cycle?" Adam curiously repeated. "You mean like steroids?" Adam asked hesitantly.

Jason's eyes gleamed. "Yeah, gear. Juice."

Adam nodded, "Like fina–"

"Wait, how do you know about finaplix?" Jason curiously replied.

"I made some," Adam confessed. "But I ended up getting an infection."

Jason chuckled, shaking his head.

"A fuckin' abscess!? That's why you passed out, right?"

Adam nodded. "Yeah, then my girlfriend threw all my shit away."

Jason's expression hardened. "My girl knows better than that shit. Don't worry she'll be okay with it when you're fucking her three times a day, and she can't walk anymore." The two of them laughed, but Adam's laugh felt hollow, weak.

Jason clapped him on the back, writing something on a piece of paper.

"Let's get you on some clean, state-of-the-art shit," he said, handing Adam his email.

"Hit me up if you want to stop by and get educated."

"This is your email." Adam questioned.

"Yeah I don't give my phone number out to strangers dude." He smirked and threw up a peace sign as he walked away.

Adam watched him disappear into the darkness, then looked down at the piece of paper in his hand before sliding it into his pocket.

Sara's words echoed in his mind, each one cutting deeper than the last. "You're done with this shit, Adam! Adam Stop! You're hurting me..."

He swallowed hard, the weight of her voice pressing against his chest. Maybe she was right. Maybe taking a break from the gear wouldn't just be okay—it would be necessary.

Setting thoughts of Sara and the pressure she had placed on him aside, Adam's stomach churned with a mix of nerves and determination as he approached the gym doors. He paused for a moment, taking a deep breath, trying to summon the courage to face it all again. He took a deep breath, lowered his hoodie and stepped inside.

The musty gym air hit him and he smiled a little. He missed that smell. But what he didn't miss was the cunt working the front desk. The same rude one who barely could look at him. Tonight was no different.

When she finally noticed him, her lips curled into a faint smirk, followed by a soft giggle, as if she was embarrassed for him to even be there.

"Scan your code," she said flatly, not bothering to meet his eyes.

Adam shakily held out his key tag, but the scanner let out a harsh beep. Rejected. He tried again. Beep. Rejected. She sighed dramatically, her annoyance palpable.

"It's not working."

"Can you try my phone number or something?" Adam

asked hesitantly, his voice low.

The situation couldn't get any worse. He already felt self-conscious coming back after the accident, and now a small line of people was forming behind him. All of them were watching.

Rolling her eyes, she snatched his tag and began typing the information manually. Finally, the system dinged, accepting the code. Without a word, she handed it back, her face blank with disinterest.

"Thanks," Adam muttered, grabbing the tag and walking past her without looking back.

The gym was as crowded as ever, filled with the hum of treadmills, the clanging of weights, and scattered bursts of conversation. Adam made his way to the treadmill section, deciding to ease into it with a slow jog. As he moved, the nagging pain in his injured ass cheek flared with every step, each jolt a reminder of the damage he was trying to ignore.

After a few minutes, he moved to the chest press machine, determined to push through the pain and rebuild. Adjusting the seat and setting a light weight, he positioned himself carefully. He gripped the handles, took a steadying breath, and pressed.

The moment he applied force, a sharp pain ripped through his lower body, shooting down into his ass. It was as if the scar itself was splitting open. He froze, the sensation so intense it took his breath away. It wasn't just physical—he knew that much. The pain lived in his mind now, entwined with his fear and self-doubt, tightening its grip on him.

Adam sat there, his hands gripping the handles, knuckles white, his breath coming in uneven gasps. He tried again, pushing against the weight, but his arms shook violently, and the sharp jolt of pain shot through him once more. His muscles betrayed him, refusing to cooperate.

He glanced around—no one seemed to notice, thankfully—but it didn't matter. The failure wasn't for them to see. It was for him to feel. He wasn't ready for this. He wasn't ready to be weak again.

Back at his apartment that night, Adam sat naked on the cold bathroom floor, his phone in one hand. His gym clothes were crumpled next to him. He didn't know what he was doing anymore.

His phone was still playing the porn video he'd turned to out of frustration. But nothing was working—not his flaccid dick, not his mind.

He had been trying to get off for nearly an hour, and he couldn't even manage that. His muscles felt weak, useless, like they were betraying him. His mind was foggy, lost in a haze of doubt and shame.

He slammed the phone down, disgusted with himself.

"Fuck this," he muttered, the word hanging heavy in the air.

Adam drew his knees to his chest, his eyes stinging with unshed tears.

"What is wrong with me?"

He'd never felt this out of control, this powerless. The memory of passing out at the gym, of Sara peeling off that bandage, of Jason's easy confidence—everything was too much for him, it all felt suffocating.

"Let's get you on some clean, state-of-the-art shit."

Jason's words echoed in his head, gnawing at him. He closed his eyes, but all he could see was that scar—a symbol of his body's weakness etched into his skin, a permanent reminder of his failure. And now, even Sara didn't look at him the same way. She said the right things, sure, but deep down, Adam could tell she wasn't attracted to him like she used to be. He'd catch her glancing at him with concern, but there was something else there too—pity.

He couldn't take it anymore.

Adam grabbed his gym pants from the floor and rummaged through the pocket. His fingers brushed against the small slip of paper. He hesitated for a moment, then, with trembling hands, unfolded it. Jason's email address stared back at him.

If he went through with this, everything could change.

Or maybe nothing would. He wasn't sure anymore. But the thought of staying like this, weak and broken, was unbearable.

Before he could second-guess himself, his fingers typed out a short message.

Hey, it's Adam. I'm in.

His thumb hovered over the send button, and for a second, the doubt crept in again. But the memory of Jason's confidence, the promise of getting back his strength, of getting back some semblance of control over his life—it was too tempting. Adam pressed send.

The message disappeared, and Adam's stomach tightened. He felt both terrified and relieved. There was no turning back now.

CHAPTER 12

Adam stood outside Jason's house a couple of days later, his heart pounding in his chest. The neighborhood was quiet, suburban, with neatly trimmed lawns and identical houses lined up in a row. But Adam couldn't shake the feeling that he didn't belong here. He wiped his sweaty palms on his jeans, taking a deep breath before knocking on the door.

For a moment, there was silence. Then the door swung open, and Adam was greeted by a sight that caught him off guard. Jason's girlfriend stood in the doorway, dressed in a tiny bikini, her muscular frame both intimidating and impressive. She was a bodybuilder too, clearly living the lifestyle just as much as Jason.

"Hey, you must be Adam," she said, smiling. "He's just putting away the dogs. Come in."

Adam stepped inside cautiously, feeling out of place in the pristine, yet sparsely furnished home. The living room was neat but bare, with only a few pieces of cheap furniture scattered around. He noticed a couple of medals hung beside various pictures of Jason on the wall. On the table, a large bong sat next to a gallon jug of water and a collection of pill bottles.

"Can I get you anything?" she asked, as she sat down on a chair and began rolling a joint.

But before Adam could answer Jason's voice boomed from another room.

"Sit! Stay!" Adam heard dogs barking and then the sound of footsteps.

Jason appeared, grinning as usual, a ball of energy and testosterone.

"Yo! Adam, glad you made it."

He walked over, clapping Adam on the back with enough force to make him stumble slightly.

"Did you work out today?"

Adam shook his head. "No, today is my day off."

"I wish I could take a day off, I'm in heavy prep mode right now. Got a big show coming up with a couple grand in cash prizes that has my name on it. My training and dieting is on another level."

"How do you do it all?" Adam questioned.

"It's easy, I love this shit. You will too. This will be your last day off if you are serious about this shit," Jason said with a chuckle. He then walked into his kitchen and waved Adam in.

"Check this shit out. Let's get you set up."

Jason's girlfriend gave Adam a quick smile before disappearing into the other room, joint in hand. Her thong bikini shared a little too much for Adam to feel comfortable. She was muscular but perfectly feminine still. She was hot and knew it.

"Damn baby put on some clothes, you makin' our guest uncomfortable!" Jason yelled out towards her laughing. "She's in prep too–gonna jump on stage and blow the fitness class out the fuckin' water. Getting her pro card this year." He bragged to Adam.

"That's cool–pro card huh?" Adam nervously replied.

"Yup. Now get in here, let me show you some shit." Jason demanded.

Adam stepped into the kitchen, his pulse quickening as his eyes darted to the counter. It was a chaotic spread of everything he had expected—and worse.

Scattered across the scratched surface were vials of

golden liquid, some open, some still sealed. Syringes, both new and used, lay in a haphazard pile beside a small metal tray stained with remnants of oil. A digital scale sat in the middle, its surface dusted with white powder, surrounded by plastic baggies filled with crushed tablets and capsules of varying colors. A crumpled roll of cash peeked out from under a torn instruction sheet, its corners soaked with something dark.

Adam's stomach churned at the sight of it all.

"Jesus, man, you're like a damn pharmacy," he said, trying to keep his voice steady.

Jason laughed, clearly unfazed. "Yup! You gotta be prepared if you're serious about this shit."

Adam picked up a large needle, his hands shaking slightly.

"I don't know if I can do the injections anymore. There's the scar I gotta go around now and—."

Jason cut him off, already preparing a syringe for himself.

"We all got fuckin' scars bro! Nobody likes the injection part man but it's part of the game and it's the easiest way to get this shit in your system without hurting your liver, feel me?"

"My liver?" Adam asked, suddenly concerned. "What about an abscess?"

Jason rolled his eyes.

"You made dirty shit, that's why you got the infection. All this stuff here," he gestured to the vials, "is clean and sterile. Switch needles every time you fill, and when you shoot. And don't keep hitting the same spot on your ass. Rotate sites, otherwise, you'll get more scar tissue and that shit is a bitch.

Adam was caught off guard by the sheer intensity and depth of Jason's knowledge. He wasn't sure if it reassured him, making his return to steroids feel more calculated, or if it only confirmed that this world was far bigger, far more extreme than he was ready to accept.

"How do you know so much?"

"I'm a professional baby, I've been competing forever

now so you gotta just trust me when it comes to this shit."

With that being said, Jason started filling a paper bag with syringes.

"Alright, this is a 12-week cycle," Jason began. "Nothing crazy. Two shots of Cypionate, that's your testosterone, per week. And for the bulking and joints, two shots of Deca per week. Here are the 1" needles. Draw with one needle, toss it, and then put on a new one to shoot. No air bubbles, rub it out once you're done. Otherwise, you'll get these nasty oil knots. Oh yeah and you gotta aspirate to make sure you aren't in a vein."

Adam's head was spinning. The words were all blurring together—Cypionate, Deca, oil knots—none of it was sticking.

He swallowed hard, trying to keep up.

"I think I made a mistake man— I'm sorry I just—"

Cutting him off Jason grabbed Adam by the face. His huge hands covered both sides of Adam's head.

Adam's eyes opened large in shock.

"You gotta man the fuck up! Ask yourself if you want this every time. Every time! Answer 'YES' and fucking shoot. Am I wasting my fucking time with you? I invite you to home, you see all my shit and what I'm just gonna let you walk bro?"

Adam pulled away.

"No... I mean I'm cool man–"

Jason thought for a second, glancing over at the scared Adam, and decided on what to do.

"Alright listen, I'm taking my shots today. I'll show you how I do it."

They relocated to Jason's bathroom where he had his pants down, ready to take his shots. Adam stared apprehensively at his muscular butt cheek. You could see the ripples of the muscle fibers and his veins through his hamstring and quads. His skin was paper thin.

"Okay, once the syringe has no air bubbles, you put 1 thumb on your hip and make an L. That's where you shoot." Jason then made the L, winded up and shot himself with the needle. They both watched as the oil went in and Jason withdrew. A line of oil snuck out of the small wound and Adam who was already sweating looked close to fainting.

Jason rubbed the oil knot and pulled up his shorts.

"No blood equals no vein and only muscle. No big deal right?"

Adam shook his head too fast. "Ugh I'm going to be sick."

Jason grabbed him by his shoulders.

"Stop this shit. You are a grown ass man who is about to become a grown ass beast. Right?"

Adam slowly nodded, like he had a choice.

"Now I have to do another one in my shoulder. Watch."

Jason expertly filled another needle, flicked the air bubbles out and shot it in his shoulder. As he slowly pushed the oil inside of him Adam looked away. This time Adam fell to his knees relying on his grip on the bathroom counter from hitting the ground..

"Yo you going to be alright bro?" Jason asked, putting a hand out to help him back up.

"Yeah, give me a few minutes." Adam whispered.

Jason threw away his needles and helped Adam out of the bathroom. They walked back to the living room and sat on the couch.

Jason's girlfriend, now dressed in some boy short underwear and a tank top came over and started rubbing Jason's shoulder for him. She then packed him a bong rip and handed it to him. Jason offered it to Adam first.

"I'm good, I don't smoke." Adam declined.

Jason chuckled, "You will dude. Pain from the workouts and this shit will give you headaches sometimes too."

Jason took a long rip and passed the bong to his girlfriend who did the same.

"So. What is this cycle costing me? My dad always taught me nothing is free," Adam asked Jason.

"Your dad is a smart man." Jason started to answer when his phone rang and he picked it up.

"Who's this? Oh shit. What's up big man. Yeah how

much? I got it all, player. T, D, Balls, Fin, Winny. Okay. Time to get lean huh?"

Jason looked up at Adam and smiled slowly.

"All good, get the money ready, I'll have my associate bring it by in due time."

Jason hangs up and looks at Adam.

"I need you to deliver some stuff. You take this to my guy, get my money, and I'll cover your first cycle. No cost to you."

"Hold on a minute. Just wait. Who?" Adam blurted. Shocked by the idea of now becoming a delivery boy.

"Just deliver this gift bag to a client and I won't charge you for the gear." Jason snakily replied.

"I don't know man, maybe I have enough money to just pay for my shit."

Jason raised his hands up in surrender.

"That's cool. Okay 3 bottles of test and 3 bottles of deca. So $1200 and I'll throw in the pins."

"$1200 for real!?" Adam practically yelled.

"Yeah, $200 a bottle." Jason snapped back.

"Damn I can't afford that—" Adam sighed.

"Well you want to blow up or nah?" Jason replied.

"Okay just to be clear here... I'm selling him steroids?" Adam uttered.

"Just think of it as medicine. I'm the doctor and pharmacy and you are the nurse."

Adam gave him a look.

"Okay fine my assistant. He lives a couple miles away." Jason jokingly replied.

Adam stared at the ground, weighing his options. He couldn't afford the steroids on his own. That much was clear. But getting involved in Jason's world, delivering drugs to some random guy—it felt wrong. Dangerous.

"Come on, man. It's easy money," Jason said, handing him the paper. "Drop it off, get the cash, and you're set. No strings attached."

Adam was about to step off a cliff, and he wasn't sure if he could stop himself.

"Here take your shit with you, I gotta put together our customer's bag. I'll email you when it's ready."

Jason pushed the $1200 brown paper bag of steroids into Adam's chest and smiled big.

Adam's head buzzed with the weight of everything. His feet moved automatically, but his mind was racing, jumping between the $1200 price tag Jason had slapped on the steroids and the thought of what Sara would say if she knew what he was about to do.

Inside his dim apartment, Adam stood frozen, thinking of what he had basically agreed to. It seemed so simple, but it felt heavier than anything he had carried before. He could hear Sara bustling in the kitchen, unaware of what he had just agreed to. Part of him wanted to return his steroids to Jason and tear the paper bag up, pretend it never happened. But that old familiar itch—the one that craved strength, confidence, power—was there, whispering in the back of his mind.

He couldn't stay like this and he would do whatever it took to make sure he didn't. He looked at the address one more time and made peace with it. He was going to deliver steroids for Jason.

CHAPTER 13

Adam stood in front of the bathroom mirror, staring down at the bag sitting on the counter. His hands were clammy, his heart racing. He couldn't believe he was doing this again. After everything that had happened, all the promises he'd made to Sara and to himself. And yet here he was. Back where it all started.

He pulled the bottles from the bag, carefully placing each one on the counter. The needles came next, along with a piece of paper that had Jason's messy handwriting scribbled across it.

Half a CC of Deca, 1 CC of Test.

Simple instructions, yet they weighed heavy on him.

Adam picked up the syringe and held it for a moment, feeling the cool plastic against his fingertips. He took a deep breath. This was it. If he did this, there was no going back, but the desire to feel powerful again, to feel like his old self, was too strong. It ate at him, made him feel weak without it.

"Okay," he muttered under his breath, trying to psych himself up.

"Thumb on the hip. Make an L." He positioned his hand over his left butt cheek, just like Jason had taught him. His fingers trembled slightly as he tried to find the right spot.

"Shit," Adam whispered. He realized his hands were

smaller than Jason's. What if he was off by an inch? What if he hit the wrong spot? What if he got another abscess? The anxiety twisted in his gut, but he pushed it down. He couldn't allow those weak thoughts to control him anymore.

He adjusted his hand, marking a spot that felt right. His reflection stared back at him, pale and uncertain.

"How bad do you want this?"

The question hung in the air, his voice a soft echo against the tiled walls. He needed this. He needed to be strong again, to prove to himself and to everyone else that he wasn't weak. The humiliation of passing out at the gym still haunted him. This was his way back.

He steadied the needle, ready to push it into his flesh once again when the bathroom door creaked slightly.

"Adam, are you in here?" Sara's voice was muffled, but it jolted him like a slap to the face. His heart rate spiked. He couldn't let her see him like this, not again.

"Yeah!" Adam yelled back, panic rising in his throat. "I'm, uh, taking a shit. Be out in a minute."

Sara paused on the other side of the door.

He glanced at the syringe, his fingers trembling again.

"Sara, just... give me a second, okay?"

There was silence for a long minute. He could hear her shifting, probably standing with her arms crossed, suspicious.

"I don't believe you," she said softly, the hurt in her voice cutting through the thin door. "If you're doing steroids—"

Before she could finish, Adam shoved the needle into his skin, pushing it deep into his muscle. A sharp pain shot through his body, but he gritted his teeth and ignored it. He couldn't let her stop him. Not now.

His thumb pressed the plunger, injecting the oil into his body. It burned, but it was a familiar pain, one he welcomed. The pain meant he was getting stronger. The pain meant it was working.

Adam pulled the needle out quickly, tossing it into the sink. He rubbed the injection site, trying to work the oil into his muscle. His heart pounded in his chest as he looked at himself in the mirror and quickly pulled up his underwear. Fighting back the nausea that came with his injections he turned on the water and splashed his face a little.

"Adam." Sara's voice now sounding tired and defeated.

"Shit." He mumbled to himself trying to pack everything away.

He glanced down, a damp sensation catching his attention. A small spot of blood had seeped through his boxers, marking the spot where the needle had pierced his skin.

"Fuck," he muttered, grabbing a tissue to wipe it away. He needed to get out there before Sara pushed any harder.

And he did, quickly leaving the bathroom, not even bothering to put his pants back on. The loose fabric of his boxers flapped against his legs as he walked into the living room, where Sara was throwing clothes into a bag.

"Where are you going?" Adam asked, trying to keep his voice calm, but he could hear the strain in his words.

Sara didn't look up. "We talked about this, Adam. No more steroids. You don't need them. For fuck's sake, you've never needed them!"

"I'm not doing steroids," Adam lied, his voice coming out too quickly, too defensive. "I was taking a shit."

Sara stopped packing for a second and looked at him. Her eyes were tired but burning with anger.

"Do you think I'm stupid?"

Adam tried to hold her gaze but faltered. "No, I just—"

"Yeah, you must," she interrupted, her voice rising slightly. She pointed at the bloodstain on his boxers.

"I can see the damn blood on your underwear, Adam. Stop fuckin' lying to me!"

Adam looked down at the small red spot, his stomach twisting. "Okay yes," he muttered under his breath. He tried to recover, raising his hands in defence.

"Babe, these are different. They're better. Cleaner."

Sara scoffed, turning back to her bag. "No, they're

not. You need help Adam. So either throw them out, or I'm gone for good this time."

Adam's chest tightened. "What? Wait, wait a minute. Isn't that a little harsh? I'm doing this for us!"

"For us?" Sara spun around, her eyes flashing with anger.

"You're doing this for us? You mean like the last time when you almost died? You have only ever done that shit for one person, Adam. And that's you! You never once cared about what I would think or your parents."

Adam flinched at her words, but he tried to hold his ground.

"Look, a friend at the gym hooked me up. These are safe, Sara. They are top-of-the-line, not like the wack stuff I used to take. I just have to help him out with some things and he'll give them to me for free, but it's no big deal."

Sara's hands froze mid-pack. She looked at him, her expression shifting from anger to concern.

"Help him with what?"

Adam hesitated, running a hand through his hair. "Deliveries," he muttered, barely audible.

Sara's face twisted in disbelief.

"Deliveries? Oh, so now you're his errand boy?"

Adam's throat felt tight.

"No..."

Sara shook her head, disbelief etched into every line of her face.

"So you're a drug dealer? I mean what the fuck Adam—I can't with you." Sara wiped the tears from her eyes and zipped up her bag.

Adam couldn't respond. His mind was racing, but nothing he could say would make it better.

She slung the bag over her shoulder and brushed past him, her voice ice-cold.

"Let me know when Adam is back, if he ever does."

Before Adam could say anything, the door slammed shut, the sound echoing in the empty apartment.

He stood frozen in place, his heart pounding in his

chest. The reality of what had just happened crashed over him like a tidal wave, leaving him breathless. The person he loved, the one he had convinced himself that he was doing this for, was gone. And it was his fucking fault.

"Fuck!" Adam screamed, punching the air as if it could somehow release the anger and frustration building inside him. His words bounced off the walls, hollow and meaningless. Then the anger came. He was angry at him having to hide anything he was going to do. He was angry at himself for letting himself get weak again. But he was furious over the audacity of her leaving.

"Fucking bitch!" he shouted at the closed door. "Judging me for trying to be stronger, to look better. What the fuck does she know? Fucking cheating bitch! Go fuck someone else, see if I care!"

His anger boiled over, his face red, veins popping in his neck as he stormed back to the bathroom. He slammed the door behind him, the force rattling the cheap frame. He stood there, breathing heavily, his chest heaving, staring at his reflection in the mirror.

He felt trapped—trapped by his own body, by his own decisions. He wiped his face, trying to pull himself together, but the frustration remained. He needed to do something, anything to clear his mind. So he went to the gym.

Adam sat on a bench in the back corner of the gym, his oversized shirt sticking to his sweat-soaked skin. His heart raced, his muscles twitching as he wiped the sweat from his brow. The weight on the bar wasn't heavy, but it felt like lead in his hands. He needed to push harder, to feel the burn.

The scar still mentally yelled at him. Reminding him of the failure he was, the embarrassment that was before. But that was before. He was weak. He was taking dirty shit as Jason said. And Jason was right, this new stuff, this first shot felt good. He could taste it even.

The mirror in front of him showed a man who still wasn't enough. He didn't fill out his oversized shirt anymore and no matter how hard he worked, or how much he lifted, he couldn't shake the feeling of inadequacy that chewed at his insides. He was weak.

Breaking away from the mirror and his thoughts he laid back on the bench, gripping the bar with trembling hands. Two 35-pound plates sat on either side, not much for someone who used to throw up much heavier weight.

He drove the bar up and down, each rep faster than the last, his muscles burning with intensity. "Ten, eleven, twelve, thirteen," he huffed under his breath, his breaths growing sharper with every count. Pushing himself to the brink of failure, he gave one final press before racking the bar with a loud, echoing slam.

He sat up, panting, his body drenched in sweat now. He caught his reflection in the mirror again, flexing his arms instinctively, trying to see if there was any improvement. But the man in the mirror still looked small, fragile.

Then, out of the corner of his eye, Adam saw Jason watching him. He stood near the squat rack, a grin plastered on his face. He gave Adam a knowing nod, pointing at him as if to say, it's working.

Adam nodded back, forcing a smile. He didn't want Jason to see the doubt creeping in. He didn't want anyone to know how scared he really was.

A few nights later in Adam's dimly lit bathroom, the familiar scent of rubbing alcohol and sweat hung heavy in the air. His work clothes lay crumpled on the floor, a reminder of the day he'd endured. But this was the only thing he cared about right now. The routine. The injection. The clean shit.

He stood in front of the mirror, his body tense as he prepared the syringe. The needle gleamed in the low light, a small but powerful tool that promised strength and control.

He filled it with the oily substance, careful to follow Jason's instructions exactly.

Once the syringe was ready, he lowered his boxers, exposing his left butt cheek. His hand moved automatically now, finding the spot with ease. He plunged the needle into his skin, gritting his teeth against the familiar sting. The oil burned as it entered his muscle, but he welcomed the pain.

Withdrawing the needle, he massaged the injection site, watching as a small bead of oil appeared and slowly rolled down his skin. He wiped it away, feeling the familiar rush of adrenaline and power surge through his veins.

CHAPTER 14

Adam quickly fell back into the familiar rhythm of being a gym rat. Every night, like clockwork, he found himself under the harsh fluorescent lights of the weight room, grinding away until his muscles gave out and his arms hung limp at his sides. The gym became his sanctuary, a place to channel his frustration, his fears, and his obsession with progress. But with that dedication came something else—a new steroid cycle, courtesy of Jason. This one was stronger, more intense, designed to push him past his previous limits. Each injection felt like a promise, a step closer to the body he had always envisioned. Yet, deep down, Adam couldn't ignore the weight of it all. The grueling workouts, the relentless pressure he put on himself, and the chemicals coursing through his veins—it all came at a cost.

He stood in front of the sink in the locker room, splashing cold water on his face. His reflection stared back at him, flushed and sweaty. He was filling out his shirt more, his muscles starting to respond to the steroids. But the emptiness still lingered. He couldn't shake it, no matter how much he lifted or how many injections he gave himself.

Jason walked up behind him, clapping him on the back. "How was the workout champ?"

Adam nodded, his voice distant. "Yeah, not bad. I feel

pretty good."

Jason grinned. "That's what I like to hear. Maybe one of these days you can workout with me. See how the pros do it."

"One day." Adam smirked.

Jason laughed softly in that easy way of his and handed him a slip of paper with an address on it.

"I need you at this place once you're done here. Ask for Erick."

Adam stared at the paper, feeling the weight of what Jason was asking him to do... Again. In his head he heard Sara calling him a drug dealer. He wasn't a drug dealer. Just a guy doing his best. At least that's how he sold it to himself.

"How much should I get?" Adam asked, his voice barely audible.

"He knows," Jason replied, his voice casual.

Jason dropped a brown paper bag at Adam's feet, patted him on the back again and walked away, leaving Adam standing there, holding the slip of paper.

Adam looked down at the address: 1758 Hortense St. He finished up in the locker room and headed out to the address, wanting to be done with this errand as soon as possible.

Adam stood outside the house, his heart pounding in his chest. The first time was easy. Quick, painless, safe. Just a one time thing...

The neighborhood was quiet, with little to no traffic at this time of night but his nerves were on edge. He clutched the bag in his hand, glancing around to make sure no one was watching.

He hesitantly reached for the doorbell, his fingers trembling as he pressed it. Simultaneously, almost as if on purpose his phone buzzed in his pocket. It was Sara. He stared at her name on the screen for a second before silencing the call.

The door creaked open, and a weathered-looking African-American man peered out. He wore dark shades so his eyes were covered but Adam could tell the strange man had some mileage on him.

"Who the fuck are you?" He barked at Adam.

"Jason sent me," Adam replied, trying to keep his voice steady.

The man lowered his glasses to peer at Adam and narrowed his eyes.

"What do you have for me?"

Adam hesitated for a moment, then held up the bag. "I don't know, meds?"

The guy stretched a huge arm out and grabbed Adam by the shoulder and yanked him inside the house. Adam struggled to maintain his balance, staggering his way into the shady home.

"I'll be right back, bro. Wait here—don't touch anything," Erick said before disappearing into the house.

Adam stood awkwardly near the door, clutching the bag of steroids tightly against his chest. His eyes wandered around the space, taking in his surroundings. The house was deceptively spacious, with high ceilings and an open layout. Despite its size, the place felt neglected, the dirty carpet running through the rooms adding to its worn-down vibe.

An entryway table caught his attention, cluttered with random knick-knacks and a few bodybuilding trophies that gleamed faintly under the dim light. They seemed out of place, like relics of a time when the house had seen better days.

To his right, the living room sprawled out with little to fill it. A massive TV dominated the space, flanked by a pair of old, sagging couches that looked like they'd been through their fair share of use. The emptiness of the room only emphasized the contrast between the house's size and its lack of care.

Adam shifted uneasily, his grip tightening on the bag. The longer he stood there, the more the place seemed to echo the tension he felt inside.

The weathered black man called out to Adam from the living room.

"Hey white boy, come on in. Have a seat."

Adam hesitated for a moment before nervously stepping into the room. He lowered himself onto the worn couch, his movements stiff.

"Erick," the man said, extending his hand out.

"Adam," he replied, shaking Erick's hand, trying not to show the unease bubbling beneath the surface.

Erick's massive, callused palm dwarfed Adam's thinner fingers, the rough texture digging into his skin. The force of the squeeze sent a sharp sting through Adam's hand, making him wince internally as he tried to keep his expression neutral.

"Here you go brother Adam, it's all there." Erick handed him the envelope. Adam peeked inside seeing cash and handed the steroid bag to him.

Erick looked in the bag and broke out into a big smile and quickly got to preparing his shot right there on the couch next to Adam.

"My stock ran out days ago, I've been calling Jason ever since but that fucker never answers. He always delivers quality stuff though."

Erick spoke as he flicked the air bubbles out of a fully filled syringe.

He looked over at Adam with a half smile on his face.

"I see that you're nervous bro but don't trip. I'm one of Jason's regulars so better get used to seeing my pretty face."

His face wasn't so pretty. Erick was basically a huge mass of muscle. He was entirely bald with smooth shiny black skin and bulging veins. He looked to be in his 50's but seemed relatively healthy.

"I can't get enough of this shit man. I know that sounds an awful lot like addiction but what can I say? It works for me. This shit right here makes me feel like a man, like I'm in control."

Adam found himself nodding along to Erick. He sort of understood the big guy.

"How did you get into it?" Adam cautiously asked.

Erick sighed deeply with a faraway look on his face.

"Oh man, I don't think we have enough time for all of that tonight but–I was a skinny kid who just wanted to get bigger and saw gains come real quick because of this." He holds up a vial.

"I got hooked and started taking it even more serious and became pro. That's actually where I met Jason, on the stage. As I started pivoting into training and less on the competing he hired me to help him get his pro card. The rest is history."

"Do you miss competing?" Adam asked, still treading lightly.

Erick continued, "Shit Adam, it was years ago now. But I do miss it. The intense workouts, the competition, the women, oh the women brother Adam. You know what I miss the most though? I miss the professional level juicing. We used to go on proper cycles, 1 gram a week type of shit. Not this shit I have to do now to coast by, I was like a damn bull back then–should've seen me."

He then rubbed his massive shoulder with an alcohol wipe and slammed the needle in.

"You saved my life today white boy. Tell Jason I said that." Erick said, rubbing the oil knot in his massive delt.

"Yeah— okay cool. Uhh— nice meeting you Erick." Adam nervously replied as he stood up and turned to leave.

"Hey bro—" Erick barked.

Adam turned around.

"Next time I see you, you better be bigger. Now get the fuck out of my house!" Erick responded with a smirk.

Adam forced a nervous smile and walked out, his steps feeling heavier with each passing moment. As the front door clicked shut behind him, he let out a massive sigh of relief. But he had a gnawing sensation settled deep in his gut, twisting tighter with every breath. He was in deeper than he had ever imagined.

CHAPTER 15

Adam sat back on Jason's worn-out couch, his eyes half-lidded as the smoke from the bong curled up into the air. He felt the heaviness of it settling into his chest, the familiar haze beginning to cloud his thoughts. His body felt warm, relaxed. Jason, on the other hand, was all business, hunched over a wad of cash, counting it with the precision of someone who had done this a thousand times before.

Jason suddenly stopped, looking down at the stack of bills with a frown.

"What the fuck, bro?" Jason said, his voice serious. "This is short."

Adam coughed, the smoke catching in his throat as he looked up in confusion. "What? I did exactly what you—"

Before he could finish, Jason broke into a grin, slapping Adam on the back.

"Ahh, I'm fucking with you!" Jason laughed.

Adam choked on the smoke again, his heart racing from the sudden panic.

"Not funny, man," he muttered, taking another hit to calm himself down.

Jason chuckled, leaning back into the couch.

"Relax, bro. I'm making some good money now. Must be bulking season or some shit."

He turned his gaze toward Adam, his eyes narrowing in on him like a coach sizing up a player.

"Stand up," Jason said. "Let's get a look at you."

Adam shook his head, sinking deeper into the couch cushions.

"Nah, man. I'm high as hell right now. Another day—"

Jason wasn't having it.

"Come on, dude. This is free bodybuilding advice. You know how much people pay for this shit?"

Reluctantly, Adam sighed and stood up. His legs felt heavy, and his muscles ached from the latest injection, but he peeled off his shirt and tossed it onto the couch. The cool air hit his skin, and he flexed instinctively. He wasn't where he wanted to be, but he could see the progress. His shoulders were broader, his chest more defined. But there were downsides too—small clusters of acne dotted his back and shoulders now, a reminder of what was coursing through his veins.

Jason nodded approvingly, his eyes studying every muscle fiber. "Nice. Your delts are coming in strong. You're looking good, man. Feel like a pin cushion yet?"

Adam gave a weak laugh. "Dude, my ass is always sore."

"Part of the game. Throw your shirt back on before my girl sees you, don't want her leaving me for a younger man."

Adam looked over at Jason laughing hysterically.

Adam chuckled a little, put his shirt back on and slowly took a seat back on the couch.

"Hey man—So I'm gonna need more soon." Adam casually muttered.

Jason raised an eyebrow, suspicion flashing across his face.

"Why more? You just got some."

Adam hesitated, then scratched the back of his neck.

"Yeah, I, uh, knocked a bottle off the bathroom counter. It broke. Dumb mistake."

He was obviously lying and Jason suspected such. Jason's expression darkened for a moment, his voice low and serious.

"Look, don't be doing more than I said, alright? That shit will fuck you up. You already had an abscess, you already got some acne but the shit can get worse, way fucking worse. Bitch tits, hepatitis, heart problems. I've seen mother fuckers die bro!"

Adam nodded quickly. "I know, I know. I'm sticking to what you told me. Promise."

Jason leaned back into the couch, his demeanor softening. He took another hit from the bong and passed it back over to Adam.

"Grab a bottle of test before you leave, just don't waste it this time."

Adam took the bong from Jason, inhaling deeply. His head felt light, his thoughts drifting.

"Yeah, for sure. It's getting late anyway," Adam said, looking toward the door. "I got work in the morning."

Jason gave a lazy nod, his voice muffled by the smoke. "Coo'. See ya at the gym, bro."

Adam grabbed a bottle of testosterone from the counter on his way out. As he walked to the door, he heard Jason cough violently from another bong hit.

"Later, man," Adam called over his shoulder before stepping into the night.

Back in his house, Adam lay sprawled on his bed, eyes locked on the TV. The light from the screen flickered across his face as he lazily flipped through the channels. Nothing was holding his interest. His mind was somewhere else—floating, half-aware, still in a fog.

His phone buzzed next to him, snapping him out of it briefly. It lit up with a message from Sara. He stared at it for a long time before finally picking the phone up to read it. Her name glowed on the screen.

"Are you just going to keep ignoring me? Call me."

He clenched his jaw. His memory of her was beginning to distort, shifting into something he no longer recognized or liked. Sara was always nagging him, always pressuring him about the steroids, about their relationship, about everything. She didn't get it. She didn't understand what it was like to be a man and feel weak, to feel small. She didn't understand the obsession with growing bigger, stronger—how it had slowly consumed him whole.

Adam hit the clear button, deleting the message without a second thought. He couldn't deal with her right now.

He opened up his browser and pulled up his favorite porn site and typed in: muscle women. The fantasy of bare skin, penetration, and lean muscular bodies, the kind of cheap thrill that could distract him from everything else.

He reached under his bed, grabbing a towel he kept there for moments like this. His muscles were sore, his mind foggy, but this—this he could control. As he worked himself up, he stared at his arms, noticing how thick the veins in his forearms had become. They bulged under the skin, evidence of the steroids taking effect. He liked the result he saw and got more turned on by the thought of his new body. He reached his climax effortlessly, sinking into the lingering haze of satisfaction.

And for a brief moment, Adam grinned—the widest smile he'd had in weeks. He could see it now. The results. The veins, the muscles, the strength. The chemicals were working, transforming him. This was the payoff. And for once, it felt so fucking good to be him.

CHAPTER 16

Adam sat in his cubicle, the monotonous hum of office life filling the air around him. The fluorescent lights above cast a harsh glow on the rows of identical desks, each one occupied by someone just as bored as he was. His face had changed. It was fuller now, rounder, and there was a redness to his skin that hadn't been there before. He was starting to look more and more like the person he wanted to see in the gym mirror—that guy was bigger but also more distant from the world around him.

He clicked his mouse a few times, pulling up the next number on his list of cold calls. It was the same thing every day. Call, pitch, get rejected, move on. A rhythm of futility.

He dialed a number and waited. The phone rang a few times before an old man answered.

"Hello?" The voice on the other end was scratchy, worn down by time.

"Uh, yes, is this Mr... Gardia?" Adam's voice wavered a little, trying to sound professional.

"Yes, who is this?" the old man snapped.

Adam swallowed. "Sorry to bother you, sir, but I have a special—"

The old man cut him off. "I aint interested, boy! Now leave me–"

Adam clenched his jaw. "Well sir—"

"Let me finish!" the man barked, his voice rising with anger. "When I was your age, I was serving my country. What are you doing? Sitting there like a weak civilian, a pussy who's done nothing for his godforsaken country? Huh? Huh? I can't hear you, boy!"

Something snapped in Adam. His face turned redder, and he shouted into the phone without thinking,

"YOU KNOW WHAT!"

But he caught himself mid-sentence, realizing how loud he was. He took a deep breath and forced a smile, even though the old man couldn't see it.

"Sir, I think you're really missing out today."

"Goodbye, Nancy boy!" the old man spat just before hanging up.

The line went dead, and Adam slammed the phone down on the receiver nearly breaking it in two.

Adam sat there, seething. Normally, he could handle rude callers, but this time something was different. His heart was racing, and his hands were clenched into fists. He hadn't felt this kind of rage since–well since the awful night with Sara. He clicked his mouse again, pulling up the next number. His temples throbbed as he forced himself to calm down.

"Hola?" a voice answered.

"Uh, is this Rodriguez Ra..." Adam trailed off, struggling to pronounce the last name.

"Sí," the man on the other end replied.

Adam cleared his throat. "Okay great, how–how are you?"

There was a brief pause, and then, "¿Qué?"

Adam's grip tightened on the phone. "Sir, maybe you have a son or daughter who can help translate?" he asked, his voice more forceful this time.

"Sí." the man replied.

Another voice cut in, this one younger and more aggressive. "Hey, hello!?"

"Uh, yeah, hello?" Adam said, his annoyance growing.

"Hey, mang, who da fuck you talkin' about?" the younger voice demanded.

Adam's face burned. "I was asking if there was someone who spoke English in the house, that's all."

"You trying to sell my abuelito some bullshit? Take advantage of him. I'll look up that motherfuckin' company and find you."

Adam froze, a blank expression spreading across his face as the man kept ranting.

"Hey white boy! You fuckin' understand me, dawg? Find you foo'!" The voice on the other end was venomous.

Adam's mind raced, the rage boiling up inside him. The grandson's voice grew louder and more threatening, "DID THIS RETARDED BROKE BITCH—"

And Adam lost it. He exploded into the phone, his voice shaking with fury.

"NOW YOU LISTEN TO ME, PACO PIECE OF SPIC ASS SHIT! IF YOU EVER THINK ABOUT COMING DOWN HERE, I WILL KILL EVERY SINGLE PERSON IN YOUR FAMILY. MAN, WOMAN, CHILD, I DON'T GIVE A SHIT, AND MAKE YOU WATCH! AND I'LL SAVE YOU FOR LAST! YOU HEAR ME? YOU UNDERSTAND ME, DAWG?"

The phone line went dead, the dial tone buzzing in his ear.

Adam blinked, his heart hammering like a drum in his chest. He slowly lowered the phone to the desk, realizing that everyone in the office had heard him. The entire floor had gone silent.

Across the room, George stood up, his jaw slack, staring at Adam in disbelief. Other coworkers whispered to each other, wide-eyed and stunned.

Then, from the corner of the office, Mr. Louis stormed out of his office as fast as his beer gut would allow him, his face red with fury. He marched straight to Adam's desk.

"What the hell was that I just heard, Mr. Stenson? That was absolutely unbelievable! Get your things and go home. I'll let you know when— if—you're ever coming back!" Mr. Louis's voice was thunderous.

Adam sat frozen for a second, still in shock over what he had just done. He quickly gathered his belongings, avoiding eye contact with the people around him.

"Everyone, back to work!" Mr. Louis barked at the office, turning back to Adam. "That is a perfect example of how to end your career here. I don't care how bad a day you are having, or how fucked up your life might be, you do not take it out of the customers!"

As Adam walked out, he saw George trying to initiate a slow clap, but Mr. Louis shut it down with a single glare. "Back to work, George! Or you can head out with him right now."

George ducked down, disappearing into his cubicle as Adam walked past.

Back at home, Adam stood in front of his bathroom mirror, staring at his reflection. His face was still flushed from the day's events, his jaw tight with anger. He couldn't believe what had happened. He had lost it, completely blown up, and now he was probably out of a job. All because of some punk kid on the phone.

He gritted his teeth, pulling at the collar of his gym shirt. His muscles pressed against the fabric, the shirt fitting him better than anything he used to wear. He glanced down at the bathroom counter, where his vials of steroids were neatly lined up. The syringes sat next to them, gleaming under the harsh bathroom light.

He flexed his arms in the mirror, watching the muscles ripple beneath his skin.

His eyes dropped to the needles. Two weren't going to be enough. Not tonight. He needed more. Needed to feel stronger. Bigger. He grabbed a third syringe, filling it up with the same ruthless precision he had developed over the last few months.

Without a moment of hesitation, he plunged the first

syringe into his shoulder. The needle pierced the skin, but he barely felt it anymore. This was routine now.

The second needle went into his left butt cheek. He could feel the familiar soreness where the injections had been building up, but he didn't care. The pain meant it was working.

The third syringe went into his right cheek, just above the jagged scar left from his earlier infection. He winced slightly but pushed through it, finishing the injection. He tossed the used needles into the sink, a small drop of blood pooling at the tip of one of them.

He flexed again in the mirror, watching his muscles bulge and walked out of the bathroom, feeling the adrenaline surging through his veins. This was the power he had been chasing. This was who he was now. Adam rode the adrenaline high all the way to his favorite place in the world, the gym.

He lay back on the bench, gripping the bar loaded with 225 pounds. His muscles screamed, but he welcomed the pain. With a grunt, he pressed the weight up, his veins bulging with each rep.

"Come on!" he growled to himself, his face red and covered in sweat. He slammed the bar back onto the rack, sitting up and flexing his arms in the mirror. The delts were popping, the chest thick. He was looking huge.

He moved to the dumbbell rack, grabbing the 40-pounders. He gritted his teeth, curling the heavy weight, sweat pouring down his face. He wasn't just working out anymore. This was war, and his body was the battlefield.

As he finished his set, he ran his hand through his hair, feeling something strange. He glanced down and saw a few strands of hair in his palm. His heart skipped a beat.

"What the fuck?" he muttered, staring at the loose hairs. He rubbed his head again, more hair coming loose and falling to the ground. He quickly glanced around to make sure nobody saw him. Adam tried to shake it off, it must have been a fluke he thought.

He moved to the rowing machine, where he loaded the stack and pulled with all his strength. But even as he strained against the machine, his mind kept drifting back to his hair. He kept it out of his mind till he got home and hopped in the shower.

The hot water poured over Adam as he stood under the showerhead, rinsing the sweat from his body. He ran his hands through his hair again, only to watch more strands fall into his hands.

Adam stared at the hair in his hands, a sinking feeling settling in his gut. He rinsed his hands under the water, watching the strands swirl down the drain.

"What the fuck is happening?" he muttered to himself. A part of him knew the ugly answer.

The steam from the shower fogged up the bathroom mirror, as Adam stepped out, he wiped it clean with one hand, staring at his reflection. His face was puffier, redder than ever. His eyes were sharper, more intense, but something felt wrong. He rubbed his scalp again, feeling the thinning patches along his hairline.

He pressed his palms against the sink, his knuckles white from gripping the counter. He was transforming, but not in the way he had imagined. The power, the muscle—it came with a price. He just didn't realize how steep that price could be.

A week of workouts and shots had passed since and the changes were getting harder to ignore. Adam stood in front of the mirror, staring at his reflection. His beard was thicker now, covering the lower half of his face. He had never had a beard before. His hair had been cut short—military style—an attempt to hide the receding hairline that seemed to worsen each day.

His skin had taken on a reddish hue, and his body, while muscular, was puffier than ever. There was a permanent tightness in his face, his features pulled taut as if he was always angry. And acne covered his shoulders and back in angry purple clusters.

Adam ran his hand over his scalp, feeling the faint remnants of his hairline. The steroids were doing what they promised—he was bigger, stronger—but the side effects were more visible than ever.

On the counter in front of him, four syringes lay neatly in a row, the vials of steroids beside them. His hands shook as he picked up the first needle.

Without hesitation, Adam jabbed the syringe into his shoulder, feeling the familiar sting. He pressed the plunger, injecting the oily substance into his muscle. He didn't feel the burn anymore. His body was used to it now.

He moved on to the next needle, jabbing it into his left butt cheek. Then the next one into his right cheek, his skin bruised and tender from weeks of injections.

As he reached for the final needle, he stopped himself. This wasn't just about getting big anymore. It had become something darker, something that was starting to take over his life.

He flexed in the mirror, his veins popping beneath the surface. "This is what I'm talking about," he whispered, trying to convince himself that this was still worth it.

But as he glanced down at his chest, something caught his eye. His nipples… they looked different. He touched them gingerly, feeling a slight tenderness. His stomach dropped.

"Bitch tits."

Jason's voice echoed faintly in his mind, warning him about the dangers of taking too much. The swelling around his nipples was faint, but it was there.

He shook his head, trying to push the thought away. He grabbed the final syringe and plunged it into his skin, feeling the familiar rush of adrenaline that came with each injection.

He flexed again in the mirror, admiring the size of his arms, the thickness of his chest. But something inside him was unsettled. He could feel the power coursing through him, but it was starting to feel less like control and more like chaos.

After his shots, Adam sat in his underwear on the edge of his bed, phone in hand. The faint light from the living room filtered into the bedroom, casting shadows on the walls.

He had been distant from Sara for weeks now. Ever since the steroids had consumed his life, their relationship had been pushed aside. She wasn't staying with him anymore, and he had no idea where she was. Up until now, he hadn't even cared enough to ask. But tonight was different. He felt peace with his body and frankly he was tired of jerking off all the time. He wanted to show her how he can please her better than ever.

He stared at the screen for a moment before typing out a message.

"I'm sorry I've been distant the past couple of weeks. I love you and I'm ready to work on this."

He hit send and waited, his heart pounding in his chest. It didn't take long for her to reply.

"Do you want me to come over and we can talk about it?"

Adam smiled faintly, a sense of relief washing over him. He quickly typed out a reply.

"Yes. I would love that."

He tossed the phone onto the bed and stood up, pacing around the room. His body felt tense, electric with energy. He was ready to see her again, to prove to her that things could be different. That he could be different.

The doorbell rang not too long after, snapping Adam out of his thoughts. He had been sitting near the front door, waiting for her to arrive. He quickly stood up, adjusted his gym pants and patted down his beard.

He opened the door, and there she was. Sara stood in the doorway, her eyes scanning him from head to toe.

"You look..." she began, her voice trailing off.

"Great, right?" Adam cut in, a smug smile on his face.

Sara frowned slightly, stepping into the apartment.

"I was going to say different," her hand brushing over his head, her fingers grazing his short hair. She touched his beard, her expression softening for a moment.

"You've changed."

"I missed you," Adam said, his voice lower now as he leaned in, his lips brushing against her neck. His hands found her waist, pulling her closer.

"Whoa," Sara said, laughing nervously. "I missed you too, but I thought we were going to talk."

Adam didn't answer. His body was humming with energy, his mind clouded with the thought of her. He pressed himself against her, kissing her neck more aggressively, his hands grabbing her ass.

Sara shifted in his arms, still trying to keep things calm.

"Adam, I thought we were—"

"I told you I missed you," Adam interrupted, his voice husky as he kissed her again, his erection pressing against her.

They locked eyes for a brief moment, and then everything exploded. They went at it, tearing off clothes, their frustration and desire coming to a head. They needed this. They needed each other, if only for a moment.

They fell onto the bed, tangled in sheets, their bodies pressing together. Adam moved quickly, his hands rough, his lips demanding. He positioned himself on top of her, their breathing heavy and synchronized.

"Fuck me Adam," Sara whispered, her voice breathy with desire.

Something snapped in Adam's mind at those words. Maybe his last line of control finally disintegrated and Adam lost himself? Maybe it was the drugs? Or maybe this new Adam was a fuckin' beast in bed. He immediately flipped her over onto her stomach, positioning her for doggy style.

His hands gripped her hips tightly leaving red marks on her soft skin as he forcefully penetrated her. She yelped in discomfort but that only energized Adam as he drove into her with unrelenting force, sending her tumbling forward, but he didn't stop—he followed, pressing down, taking control. Thrusting harder and harder. It was no longer about pleasure. It was about Adam proving something to her, to George, to himself.

"Adam, slow down," Sara said, her voice tinged with discomfort.

But he didn't hear her. Or maybe he didn't listen. His thrusts became more forceful, more erratic. His fingers gripped her hair, pulling hard as he continued to pound into her.

"Okay Stop! You're hurting me!" Sara's voice was louder now, panic seeping in. She tried to pull away, but Adam held her tighter, his grip ironclad.

Then, out of nowhere, she hit him. Her hand flew back, slapping him across the face, jolting him out of his frenzy.

Adam stopped, frozen for a second, his mind trying to process what had just happened. She had hit him and Adam transformed into something else, something scary.

Adam flipped her onto her back, his hands moving to her throat. He gripped her neck, his eyes blazing with anger as he forced himself back into her and thrusted again, harder than before. His face twisted into something cruel, something unrecognizable.

Sara gasped, her hands clawing at his wrists, her face contorted in pain. Her eyes fluttered, her breath growing shallow as he choked her.

Adam couldn't stop. His look was animalistic, his face red with blood and anger, beads of sweat dripped down his forehead. He was punishing her, taking out every ounce of frustration, and pain. His mind was gone, replaced with a dark, primal need for dominance.

Sara's eyes began to close, her body going limp beneath him. Adam didn't care, he was close, too close to stop. His orgasm hit him like a freight train, his body shuddering like a downed bull as he finished inside her. Empty and exhausted he rolled off of her, his chest heaving, sweat soaking his skin.

Sara lay there for a moment, gasping for breath, tears spilling down her cheeks. She scrambled to her feet, her voice shaking as she pulled on her clothes.

"It's over! I'm a fool for coming here," she said through sobs, her voice cracking with emotion. "You sick fuckin' pig!"

She rushed toward the door, grabbing her things as she moved. Adam, still catching his breath, sat up, his face twisted with rage.

"Isn't this what you wanted? To be fucked by a real man?!" He roared at her.

Without a second glance, she yanked the door open and rushed out of the apartment.

Adam stood there, naked and frozen. His breathing was ragged, his chest heaving as he tried to make sense of what had just happened. His muscles, swollen from the thrusting and adrenaline, twitched with tension.

Adam stared at the open door, the empty hallway beyond it swallowing the echoes of Sara's departure. His heart raced, pounding so hard in his chest he could hear it in his ears. Sweat dripped from his brow, and his body felt heavy, drained not just from the physical exertion but from the emotional weight of what had just occurred.

"What the fuck did I just do?" Adam muttered under his breath, rubbing a hand over his face, the reality of the situation sinking in like a cold punch to the gut.

"What the fuck did I just do?"

CHAPTER 17

Adam stood in his cramped kitchen, his bare torso flushed an unnatural red from the steroids coursing through his system. His once smooth skin was now riddled with inflamed acne, a glaring testament to the hormonal chaos raging within him. His nipples appeared swollen, puffier than they should be, and a constant sheen of sweat clung to his body, no matter how cool the room was.

The faint sizzle of eggs frying in the pan cut through the quiet of the morning. He moved mechanically, flipping the eggs, his mind clearly elsewhere.

His phone buzzed on the counter. He glanced at the screen—Mr. Louis.

Reluctantly, he picked it up.

"Hello," Adam answered, his voice flat.

"Mr. Stenson," the voice on the other end said, businesslike and cold.

"Mr. Louis?" Adam asked, already knowing the answer.

"Yes," Mr. Louis confirmed. There was a pause, the kind that always filled Adam with a dull dread. "I think you've had long enough to think about what happened. Are you ready to come back?"

Adam let out a breath, the tension in his chest loosening slightly. "Yeah, sounds good. Thanks."

"Alright. Tomorrow, 9 a.m. sharp. Come to my office immediately when you clock in."

"Okay, thanks." Adam hung up.

The relief that washed over him was short-lived, replaced almost instantly by a creeping sense of doom. He thought of Mr. Louis and his shit job, did he even want it back? His jaw clenched involuntarily at the thought of it.

Adam finished cooking and sat at the small, cluttered kitchen table, a fork in one hand and a headache throbbing behind his eyes. He rubbed his temples, trying to ease the pain. Nothing worked. Reaching into a nearby drawer, he pulled out a joint, lit it, and took a long drag, exhaling with a slow, satisfied grin. The tension in his muscles eased, if only for a moment.

After breakfast, Adam stood in his bathroom staring down at four syringes laid neatly on the countertop. He was no stranger to 4 now. It had become a ritual, 1 for each shoulder and each glute. A necessary evil to keep him going. He filled each syringe with precision, flicking them to clear the air bubbles. His hands were steady—too practiced at this by now.

One by one, the needles broke through his scarred skin with dull pops. Each injection felt like a bitter commitment, a promise to himself that he couldn't break, even if it meant destroying his body in the process.

Later that evening, the gym was packed. The familiar smell of sweat, rubber, and iron hung in the air. Adam wore a y-back tank top that showed off his full frame. The type of tank top bodybuilders wear. His skin was still angry and red, his face and body pocked with acne. But now he was big. He could feel it—really feel it. It was finally working. And for the first time, he wasn't ashamed to let it be seen.

He approached the deadlift bar, the same one he had passed out at a few months ago, and let out a deep, guttural yell as he lifted the weight, feeling his muscles strain under the effort. But this time, he didn't falter.

Across the gym, eyes were on him. The way he used

to watch others, they were now watching him. And just like he once had, they were forming their own silent judgments.

Whispers spread like wildfire across the gym, murmurs laced with curiosity, skepticism, and quiet contempt.

"Isn't that the skinny kid who almost died here?" one guy muttered to his friend, his voice barely audible over the clanking of weights. His arms strained under the dumbbells, but his attention was locked on Adam.

A few feet away, another group of gym rats had taken notice, their stares lingering, their expressions a mix of disdain and intrigue.

"That kid's juicing like crazy," one of them scoffed, shaking his head.

"I wonder what his cycle is," another chimed in, his tone laced with morbid fascination.

A third guy, unimpressed, smirked. "I could lift that shit easy."

"Stop being a hater," his friend shot back, still watching Adam with something close to admiration.

"I'm not hating. I'm just saying."

The words, though hushed, carried through the gym like an unspoken verdict. Adam was no longer invisible—but that didn't mean they respected him.

Adam let the bar crash down to the floor with a loud clang, the noise reverberating through the gym, drawing even more attention.

At that moment, Jason walked in, his presence impossible to ignore. He wore an oversized T-shirt, the fabric draping over his frame, while his weight belt was strapped tightly over it, accentuating the coveted "triangle" shape—broad shoulders tapering down to a small waist. As always, a visor sat low on his forehead, and a massive gym bag hung over one shoulder. His eyes scanned the room until they landed on Adam. Without hesitation, he started making his way over.

"Yo. You're definitely not taking the cycle I gave you," Jason said, half-joking, half-serious.

Adam smirked, his eyes glassy. "The more shit I take, the better I look."

Jason raised an eyebrow but shrugged. "Alright, man. I'm running low lately, so try to make it last."

"What do you mean?" Adam's tone sharpened.

"My connect got popped. Nothing's coming in for a while."

"Fuck, man, I'm almost out," Adam muttered, his panic barely contained.

"It's alright man. Time for your PCT anyway. Let your receptors reset, let your body recover. You'll keep some of the gains, and we'll get more in a month or two."

"A whole month off completely?" Adam's voice dripped with disbelief.

Jason nodded, stepping closer.

"That's the way the game is played, bro."

Adam watched him walk away, his stomach twisting. A month without his juice? The thought alone made his skin crawl. The rage bubbled up inside him, hot and fast. He grabbed the deadlift bar again, lifted it off the ground with a snarl, and slammed it back down, the clang echoing across the gym.

As he grabbed his towel and gym bag, ready to leave, a gym employee approached him cautiously.

"Hey, man," the employee said nervously, "you gotta re-rack that."

Adam turned, his eyes burning with fury.

"Yeah?" He glanced at the bar on the floor and then back at the employee.

"What the fuck are you going to do about it?"

The employee swallowed hard, trying to keep his voice steady. "Listen, I know your head's all clouded from roids and shit, but you can't—"

"Do you know me?" Adam cut him off, his voice a low growl.

The employee shook his head.

"Then get the fuck out of my face." Adam jabbed a finger into the employee's chest. "And you put the fuckin' weights away."

He shoved past the employee, his shoulder clipping

him hard enough to make a point as he stormed toward the front desk. As if the night couldn't get any worse, there she was—the same front desk girl who had never spared him a second glance. His blood was already boiling, and the sight of her only stoked the fire.

"Hey!" he barked.

She looked up, startled. "Can you hold on a sec?" she said to one of the 2 gym members she was chatting with, before turning her attention to Adam.

"How can I help you?" she asked, her voice trembling slightly.

"You know who I am right?" Adam asked, his voice dripping with contempt.

The girl's face reddened with confusion. "Umm... no sir, sorry," she stammered.

Adam leaned in, his voice lowering to a venomous whisper.

"I've been coming to this fucking gym for months, and every time I see you, you ignore me." He paused, a cruel smile tugging at his lips. "I just wanted to tell you that I hope you die of AIDS one day, you fucking cunt."

The girl's face crumpled in shock as tears welled up in her eyes.

Both men standing at the front desk looked at themselves in shock. One took half a step forward but the other put a strong hand on his shoulder and they both settled for scowling at the retreating Adam.

They immediately turned back to the receptionist.

"Who was that?" asked the first man, his voice was low and rough.

"He's just another roided-up meathead, with major issues. I know him, he just looks so different now," she said with her voice shaking.

"What kind of issues?" the other member inquired.

"I don't know. One time he passed out while lifting, word is he got an infection from steroids. I think he just had so much juice, his heart almost gave out. He's also been in a couple of fights with other members. I can't wait for his membership to expire so I can tell him that the gym doesn't want him to renew—he's a piece of shit."

"You've got his name?" one of the men asked.

"Uhh sure, let me check our records." She typed a few things into the computer. "You know I'm really not supposed to give out–"

Both men flashed their badges.

"Adam Stenson." She quickly responded.

One of the men writes Adam's name down.

"So you guys are cops?" asked the receptionist.

"Detectives. I'm Detective Murdock and this is my partner, Detective Castle."

Both had opted for casual attire tonight—baseball caps and jeans—for the visit, but on duty, it was a different story.

Castle, in his late 40s, was the no-nonsense type, with piercing gray eyes, always wearing his perpetually rumpled trench coat, and a commanding presence that demanded respect.

Murdock, younger, in his 30s, preferred a sharp, polished look, combining his disarming charm with an analytical mind that rarely missed a detail.

Detective Castle nodded, "What about the other guy? The one you were going to tell us about before captain asshole rudely interrupted?"

"What do you wanna know about him?" she asked coyly.

"His name, for starters," Detective Castle grunted.

"Oh—Jason, but he's cool. Did he do something wrong?" she nervously asked.

"Let me guess, is he good friends with everyone here?" Murdock responded.

"Pretty much. People like him." she replied.

"When was the last time you saw him?" Castle asked.

"I think it was a couple of days ago. He comes and goes."

"Last name." Castle reminded her.

She hesitantly looked at her computer and muttered,

"Meyers."

The next morning, Adam stood in front of his mirror, tightening the knot on his tie. He had shaved and cleaned up nicely.

He grabbed his phone and sent a quick text to Sara: "Heading to work, you can grab your stuff if you want."

He didn't feel good about what had happened with Sara but he was finally finding happiness and it coincided with her not being in his life anymore.

He grabbed his protein shaker, slung his bag over his shoulder, and walked out the door.

The office was eerily quiet when Adam walked in. Every head turned to stare at him, whispers rippling through the room like wildfire.

Adam ignored the murmurs, heading straight for the time clock with a smirk on his face. But when he swiped his card, the machine beeped with an error. He frowned, trying again. Still nothing. Frustration gnawed at him as he glanced around. Something wasn't right.

His eyes landed on Mr. Louis's office, and without thinking, he marched toward it. He knocked once, and through the glass, he saw Mr. Louis wave him in while hanging up the phone.

"Adam. You look good," Mr. Louis said, offering a smile that didn't reach his eyes. "Ready to work, I suppose?"

"Sure," Adam said, though his voice was flat.

Mr. Louis gestured toward the door. "Close the door, would you?"

Adam sat down, his gut slightly twisting. Almost warning him about what is about to happen.

From the outside, the employees watched in silence. They couldn't hear the words being exchanged, but it was clear from their body language that the conversation became tense.

Mr. Louis leaned forward, showing Adam something on his computer. Adam's posture changed, stiffening. His fists clenched.

Suddenly, Adam shot out of his chair, pointing angrily at Mr. Louis, his voice rising. Mr. Louis was yelling back, trying to regain control of the situation, but it was clear he was frightened.

Before anyone could react, two large security guards burst through the main door, heading straight for Mr. Louis' office. Inside, Adam was pacing, seething, his face contorted with rage. Then like a pitbull he grabbed Mr. Louis by the necktie, lifting him halfway out of his chair.

"You had me think you were gonna hire me back just to fire me in person?" Adam roared, his voice thick with betrayal.

Now at the office door, one of the security guards lunged for Adam, grabbing his arm. Adam shoved him off easily and continued his rant towards Mr. Louis.

"I should've killed you when I had the chance, you fat piece of—" Adam spat, his hands trembling with fury.

Both guards moved in, grabbing him by both arms and wrestling him to the floor. Adam thrashed and kicked as they tried to pin him down.

"Get the fuck off me! Fuck all of you!" he screamed, his voice raw with frustration.

The first guard barked at him, "Stop squirming, or we'll call the police!"

The second guard added, "Now let's go. It's over!"

They yanked him to his feet, his clothes torn, his face red and streaked with tears of rage.

As they dragged him past the cubicles, Adam's eyes darted around, searching for—.

"George?" he called out, his voice cracking. "Where's George?"

There was no answer. His co-workers stared at him in silence, their faces a mix of pity and fear.

"Did you know about this?" Adam shouted at them, struggling against the guards. "Did you? Fuck you all! Losers!"

The guards finally got Adam to the main door and pushed him through. The door slammed shut behind them, leaving the office in stunned silence. Mr. Louis slumped in his chair, his face pale and drenched in sweat.

Adam's hands gripped the steering wheel so tightly his knuckles turned white. His car swerved dangerously as he sped down the highway, heavy metal music blaring from the speakers. Every other car on the road became an obstacle, a target for his rage. He flipped them off one by one, as he passed.

He glanced at his reflection in the rearview mirror. His bottom lip was split, a thin trickle of blood seeping down his chin.

"Fire me, huh?" Adam growled to himself, spitting blood onto the dashboard. "Fucking faggot."

When he finally pulled into the parking lot of his apartment, his mind was still racing. He stormed out of the car and up the stairs to his door, which was slightly ajar.

"Fucking bitch doesn't even lock my door," he muttered under his breath, pushing it open.

Then he heard it—a faint, unmistakable moan. A woman's moan, Sara's moan.

Adam froze, his mind going blank for a split second. Then, like a coiled spring snapping, he bolted toward his bedroom, body slamming the door open.

"What the fuck!" Adam bellowed, his eyes wide with disbelief.

There, on his bed, was George, tangled up with Sara, both of them scrambling to cover themselves as Adam stood frozen in the doorway. Rage coursed through him, white-hot and all-consuming.

"Adam I–," George stammered, pulling on his jeans. "This is all a mistake–"

"I'm sorry, Adam," Sara whimpered, tears welling in her eyes. "I didn't mean for you—"

"Shut up, you whore!" Adam snapped, his voice shaking.

George held up his hands, trying to defuse the situation. "Hey, man, you should calm down."

Adam's fists clenched at his sides, trembling with barely contained fury.

"I thought we were friends!"

The room seemed to blur around Adam as adrenaline flooded his system. Everything was surreal, like he was moving through water.

George, not backing down, tried to reason with him. "Come on, man, relax. I don't know who you think you're talking to, but it's over bro."

That was it. The last straw.

Adam lunged forward with the force of a freight train, his fist connecting with George's face with a sickening crunch. George howled in pain, collapsing to the ground as Adam pounced on him, his fists flying in a blur of rage and violence. Each punch landed harder than the last, driven by months of frustration, anger, and betrayal. Adam didn't stop.

His knuckles broke but he kept going. Blood flew in the air with each pop. Sara's cries for him to stop were muted to the rage Adam had unleashed and then George finally stopped protecting himself and with 1 more right hook Adam finally stopped the destruction.

As George lay unconscious on the floor, his face a bloody mess, Adam stood over him, panting heavily. He wiped his bloodied knuckles on his pants and turned to Sara, who was cowering in the corner, her eyes wide with terror.

"See what you made me do?" Adam hissed, holding up his fists as if the blood was her fault. "You see?"

Sara sobbed, her voice barely audible. "I–I'm sorry, I just—"

"You what?" Adam's voice was low and dangerous. "You wanted a dirty black cock inside you? Or worse, you just wanted to embarrass me like everyone else does?!"

He took a step toward her, his eyes wild with anger, but before he could do anything more, the door burst open behind him.

"Police! Nobody move!" one of the officers shouted, his gun drawn.

Adam spun around, his hands flying up in confusion. "What the fuck are you doing in my house?"

"Hands up, son!" the officer ordered, while another knelt beside George, checking his vitals.

"We've got a late 20s black male, unconscious," the officer said into his radio. "A white male in custody, and a female in shock. Send an EMT."

Adam didn't resist as they cuffed him, his mind was numb, his body drained of energy. The officers led Adam out the door, the neighbors had begun to gather, watching the scene unfold with morbid curiosity. Adam's face was a mask of detached calm as he was shoved into the back of the squad car.

He stared out the window at the onlookers, his mind blank, his life crumbling to dust around him. He had become an animal, a creature driven by anger and hunger. Maybe he could never be Adam again.

CHAPTER 18

Adam sat on a hard bench inside the precinct, his wrists bound by handcuffs. His work clothes were torn, the once crisp suit now a ragged mess, mirroring the state of his life. The bench was cold against his back, and the officers who passed by barely looked at him. Just another day, just another screw-up.

A homeless man was being escorted through the station by a pair of officers. His smell hit Adam first—a stench so sharp it cut through the sterility of the precinct. Adam tried not to look, but he couldn't help himself. This is where I'm headed, he thought bitterly. He could already feel the cold sting of shame settling deep in his gut.

Then he saw them. His parents.

His mother's eyes met his first. She tried to smile, but it was forced—like she didn't know how to feel. His dad? His dad just looked at him with disgust, the kind that sticks to you. Adam dropped his head. If there was any chance this day could get worse, it just had.

A police officer approached Adam, clipboard in hand, his badge reflecting the overhead fluorescent lights. He was middle-aged, maybe in his forties, and wore the look of a man who had seen too much.

"George isn't pressing charges due to the circumstances," the officer said, reading from the clipboard. Adam's chest tightened. "But you should probably get a lawyer." The officer paused, as if trying to gauge Adam's reaction. "Your parents are here to take you home."

The officer crouched down and began unlocking Adam's handcuffs. The metal clicked, and as soon as the cuffs came off, Adam yanked his arms back, glaring at the officer.

"Calm down, man," the officer said, holding his hands up. "You could be sitting in a cell for a long time right now. Adultery is not tolerated. As a married man, I know how you felt... but just learn from this and stay out of trouble."

Adam's anger flared, a familiar heat rising in his chest. He couldn't stop the words from spilling out, bitter and sharp.

"Let me know what you do when you catch your wife fucking your best friend."

The officer's face hardened, but he didn't respond. Adam stood up and walked away before anything else could be said.

His mother rushed to him the moment he approached. She threw her arms around him, and despite everything, Adam let her hold him. The scent of her familiar perfume made him want to sink into her arms and pretend the last 24 hours hadn't happened. But he couldn't. His dad stood nearby, watching, arms crossed, eyes cold.

"You're lucky he didn't press charges, Adam," his dad said, his voice like gravel.

"Oh, stop it," his mother snapped, pulling away from Adam and glaring at her husband. "He's safe and free from this place. Let's go home."

Mr. Stenson grunted in response but said nothing more.

The drive home was tense, awkward silence filling the car like an invisible wall between them. Adam sat in the backseat, staring out the window, watching the city blur by. Swallowed up by anger, guilt, confusion. It all swirled together, impossible to untangle.

Finally, his father broke the silence.

"So let me get this straight," Mr. Stenson began, gripping the steering wheel tightly. "You get fired from your job—excuse me, escorted from your job—you almost beat your only friend to death, and you spend a few hours in jail all in the same day? I almost forgot the fact that your fiancé is nowhere to be found."

Adam's lip twitched. "Yeah, quite the day."

"Quite the day," his dad echoed, his voice dripping with sarcasm. He shook his head in disbelief. "What are you doing with your life, Adam?"

"Bob, not now," his mother pleaded, glancing back at Adam with worry in her eyes.

"No," his father said firmly, ignoring her. "I think now is as good a time as ever. What are you gonna do now, Adam?"

Adam shrugged, leaning back in his seat, eyes half-closed. "I don't know. Find another job. What do you think?"

"Don't get smart with me, son. I'm not a skinny black kid," his father shot back.

Adam's blood boiled. He clenched his fists.

"Doesn't matter who you are, old man."

There was a beat of silence that lasted too long to not be awkward.

"What?" His father's voice rose, his fury finally breaking through. "What did you just say?"

Without warning, his father jerked the wheel and pulled the car over, the tires screeching against the asphalt. He slammed on the brakes so hard the car jolted forward.

"We come to help you out of this shit pile you dug for yourself and this is how you act? Get out!" Mr. Stenson growled.

Adam sat up straight, looking at his father incredulously.

"Get. Out." His dad repeated, louder this time, his voice shaking with rage.

"Bob, stop it! Both of you!" his mom shouted, tears welling up in her eyes. "Adam, don't get out. Bob, start driving! You are not dropping our son—"

But Adam had already opened the door and stepped out, slamming it behind him. As he walked away, he held up his middle finger in the air, a final salute to his father. The car sped off, his mother's cries echoing faintly in the distance Adam walked along the side of the road, his hands shoved deep into his pockets, his head bowed.

The sun was beginning to set, casting long shadows over the highway. He felt alone, more alone than he'd ever felt in his life.

He pulled out his phone and dialed Jason's number. It rang once, twice, then went straight to voicemail. He tried again. This time, an automated voice cut in.

"We're sorry, the number you are trying to call has been disconnected. Please check the number and try again. Error 365."

Adam hung up. His hands shook as he hit redial. The same message. He threw the phone back in his pocket, the sense of dread in his stomach growing.

The street outside Jason's house was a picture of tranquility. The soft rustle of leaves in the breeze, the distant chirp of birds, and a group of children riding bikes painted the scene as just another normal day.

Then, the unmarked police cruiser pulled up, its engine breaking the calm like a jagged crack in glass. For a moment, the car idled at the curb, its presence an unsettling contrast to the serenity of the street. The doors opened in unison, and detectives Castle and Murdock stepped out. Their purposeful movements and watchful eyes disrupted the stillness, a clear sign that something more than suburban routine was about to unfold.

They moved cautiously, exchanging a glance as they approached the front door.

Castle, knocked hard on the door.

"This is the police! Open up!" he called out.

But they only got silence in return.

Murdock peered through the front window, his brow furrowing.

"I don't think anyone's home," he said, his breath fogging the glass.

Castle sighed, "We've got a warrant! What do you think, partner?"

"Let's kick this fuckin' door in then." He demanded.

Castle smirked a little, "We go in on three. Ready?"

Murdock nodded.

"One... two... three!" They kicked in the door, guns drawn, and rushed inside.

But when the dust settled, they stood there, confused.

The house was empty. No furniture, no drugs, nothing. Just bare walls and the hollow echo of their footsteps as they walked through the rooms. Jason had vanished without a trace.

"Shit," Castle muttered to himself.

Adam arrived at his apartment in a rideshare. The driver barely looked at him as Adam stepped out. His feet dragged along the cracked pavement as he approached the complex. He got to his front door and noticed it was cracked open. He paused, his mind racing with possibilities.

He slowly pushed the door open, cautiously stepping inside with measured hesitation. The air was eerily still, yet it carried a heavy, suffocating weight, thick and sharp.

The place was a wreck. His living room, already cluttered, was now completely trashed, furniture overturned, papers scattered everywhere. He remembered the fight with George, the way they had torn through the bedroom like a hurricane. But this? This was worse. The police must've searched the place too.

Adam's eyes fell on a small package just inside the door, partially hidden under a pile of clothes. He picked it up, flipping it over in his hands. No return address. His heart raced as he tore it open, his fingers trembling slightly.

Inside, nestled in a bed of packing peanuts, were vials, isopropyl alcohol, syringes, and labels.

Adam set the box down on the coffee table, the weight of it feeling heavier than it should.

This must be from Jason, he thought. If that's true then Jason was really gone, probably for good and now, this package in his hands was all that was left.

His eyes scanned the room some more. This place, like his life, was destroyed. He had nothing left but a box of drugs and the memories of everything he'd lost.

Adam sank onto the couch, his body sagging, overcome by exhaustion and pain. He reached for a bottle of painkillers from the coffee table, twisting the cap off and shaking a few into his hand. He chewed them dry, the bitterness spreading across his tongue as he swallowed.

Tears welled in his eyes as the weight of the last 24 hours crashed down on him. Everything was gone. Nothing would ever be the same. All that remained was that box—the only thing he had left. As the painkillers took hold, a numbing haze settled over him. His body slumped forward, and before he knew it, he drifted into unconsciousness.

CHAPTER 19

Adam jolted awake, unsure of where he was. His eyes darted around the room, trying to recognize his surroundings. He was home. His breathing was ragged, adrenaline still coursing through his veins from a nightmare he could barely remember. Then, the pain hit.

His hands throbbed like they'd been slammed in a car door. Looking down, he saw them—bruised, swollen, black and blue. It wasn't a dream after all.

"Shit," he muttered, flexing his fingers and wincing as needles of pain shot up his arms. His knuckles were cracked, the skin split in some places. He probably had a bunch of tiny fractures all the way up his hands. The fight with George came flooding back in sickening waves. Less of a fight really, he pounded George's face through the floor. His fists pounding against bone, over and over. The blood. So much blood.

He pushed himself up from the couch, every muscle in his body aching with the effort. Stretching his back, he took a slow glance around the dimly lit room. His apartment was a disaster—trash strewn across the floor, clothes tossed carelessly in every corner, and the sink overflowing with unwashed dishes. The coffee table was the worst of it. Vials and syringes lay scattered among empty wrappers and crumpled paper, a silent reminder of just how far he'd let things go.

Adam staggered into the kitchen, opening the freezer and grabbing an ice pack. He pressed it against his raw knuckles, sucking in a breath as the cold hit the bruises.

He made his way toward the bedroom, each step a harsh reminder of what he had become—a mess of swollen muscles, aching joints, and barely contained fury. His body felt too tight, stretched over the anger simmering beneath his skin. As he reached the door, it creaked open, and his breath hitched in his throat.

The bed was flipped, sheets torn and tossed everywhere. There, in the middle of the floor, was the dark, dried pool of blood. George's blood. Adam's heart hammered in his chest, a sickening mix of guilt and fury filling him. He blinked the images away, forcing himself to move on from the bedroom.

In the bathroom, the fluorescent light flickered as he stepped inside. The cabinet door hung open from the night before, and he reached for the shelf where he usually kept his stash. Empty. Every bottle was gone. He threw the cabinet door shut with a loud bang, then grabbed the empty bottles from the trash, tossing them back in with more force than needed. Useless now.

His reflection in the mirror drew his gaze. The rough stubble on his jaw made him look disheveled, and streaks of dried blood clung to his face and neck like a grim reminder of the chaos he'd endured. Puffy bags under his eyes added a wild intensity to his expression, a look of someone unraveling. Though his body was muscular, it seemed to sag, betrayed by the strain of months of abuse from the drugs he'd been pumping into it. It was a body pushed beyond its limits, struggling to endure the relentless punishment he demanded of it. This wasn't how it was supposed to go.

Out in the living room, the cardboard box lay half-open on the coffee table, its contents spilling onto the floor. He approached it, lifting out the syringes and vials he had received from Jason before his sudden vanishing act. A new batch. Jason had come through, as usual.

"Thank you, Jason," he muttered under his breath,

hands already moving automatically, familiar with the routine.

The clink of glass on metal echoed through the kitchen as he crushed pellets, measured CC's, and filled syringes. His mind was blank, he was moving on autopilot with all his focus only on the process of making more.

The oven clicked open, and Adam carefully removed the vials, setting them aside to cool. His hands shook slightly as he handled the sterile equipment, but he pressed on. He knew what he needed to do.

Detectives Castle and Murdock cruised through the suburban streets, the hum of the engine filling the silence between them. Castle gripped the steering wheel tight, his eyes scanning the road ahead. Beside him, Murdock was glued to his phone, scrolling through the call records they had just pulled up.

"Okay," Murdock said, breaking the silence. "Last call made to our guy was from a dude named Adam Stenson."

"Stenson eh? Is it who I think it is?" Castle growled.

"I have a good feeling it is. The juiced up kid at the gym." Murdock replied.

Castle grunted in response. "Let's get an address on this Stenson guy."

He picked up the receiver.

"This is Detective Castle. I need an address for a subject—name is Adam Stenson, phone number is 555-0189."

The faint crackle of the line carried the dispatcher's reply. "Copy that, Detective. Stand by while I run the information."

Castle tapped his fingers on the steering wheel, the brief pause stretching longer than he would have liked.

"Detective," the dispatcher's voice returned, precise and professional, "the address associated with that name and number is 10788 Buttonwood Dr, Apt 2A. Need anything further?"

"That's all. Thanks," Castle replied, already making a mental note of the address.

"You're welcome. Dispatch out."

Castle set the receiver down, his mind already racing ahead to what he might find at the location.

He glanced over at Murdock with a dry smile on his face. "Let's check it out."

Murdock slipped his phone into his jacket pocket as Castle pressed down on the gas. The cruiser sped through the sleepy suburban neighborhood, trees and houses blurring by. There was an unspoken intensity between the two. They'd been chasing Jason and he had almost made a perfect getaway, almost.

Adam had relocated back to the bathroom since it was time for his shots. He stood in front of the mirror, a fresh syringe in his hand. He could already feel his pulse quickening, the familiar buzz of anticipation tingling in his veins.

He had expertly positioned the needle on his butt cheek and pressed the needle against his skin, his fingers trembling slightly as he tried to feed it in. His hands were sweaty, slipping on the metal syringe. He pushed harder, the needle biting into his flesh.

"Come on," he whispered, gritting his teeth. The needle wasn't going in, his skin felt leathery and elusive to his touch. He pushed harder, the metal tip shaking as it finally broke through. The sudden pop made him gasp, the pain shooting up his back and into his arm like electricity.

"Fuck!" Adam cried out, his back arching as the liquid pushed into his bloodstream. His body convulsed, a wave of pain crashing over him. His muscles twitched uncontrollably which caused his legs to spasm, and his vision began to blur.

Blood welled up from the injection site, running down his legs and onto the tiled floor. He pulled the needle out with a grunt, tossing it aside and grabbing a towel to staunch the blood flow from the sink.

"Shit, shit, shit," he muttered, pressing the towel to the wound, trying to stop the bleeding. But it wouldn't stop. The blood kept coming, soaking through the towel, staining his fingers red.

Adam leaned against the sink, his breath shallow and ragged. He looked down at his exposed butt cheek and the ugly scar beneath it, the blood still pouring from the injection site. His mind was spinning, his heart pounding like a race-horse bolting out of control. This wasn't right.

Adam stumbled back and forth in his bathroom, knocking vials over and making a mess. Used towels sat bloodied and abandoned on the sink, his blood slowly pooling at his feet.

Adam was getting dizzy but he kept on pushing down on the towel with all the strength he could muster. A knock on the door jolted him from his frantic panicking. He froze, every muscle in his body tensing. Another knock, this time louder.

Adam's heart raced. Who the hell was at his door? He wasn't expecting anyone. He stood there in the bathroom, paralyzed, as the knocking continued, more insistent now. Finally, he moved, wiping his bloody hands on his shirt before limping his way to the door with a fresh towel pressed against his ass. He peered through the peephole, his breath catching in his throat. Cops.

Two of them. They stood there with pissed-off expressions and hands on their belts, looking as if they already knew what was behind that door.

Adam's pulse pounded in his ears. He could feel his heart struggle to pump blood but the adrenaline clouded his senses. He backed away slowly, his mind scrambling for a plan. Shit. What now?

Another knock. This time louder

"Police! Open up!"

Adam's chest tightened. He wasn't ready for this. He wasn't ready for any of this.

Detective Castle stood at the door, his partner Murdock beside him. They exchanged a glance, the tension between them thickening. Castle knocked again, this time with more force.

"Adam Stenson, this is the police. Open the door."

No response.

Murdock shifted on his feet, reaching for his holster. "You think he's in there?"

Castle nodded slowly. "Yeah. He's in there."

Adam could hear them outside, their voices muffled but unmistakable. His heart was hammering in his chest, sweat dripping down his forehead. He scanned the room, looking for any escape. The windows? No, too far up.

He had no options.

"Fuck!" he hissed under his breath, backing away from the door. His head was spinning, the blood loss making him feel lightheaded and his heart threatened to give out.

He scrambled back to the bathroom in a daze. He had already lost so much blood. Looking at himself in the mirror he could see it— he was dying. He decided to go back outside and throw himself at the feet of the cops. At least they wouldn't kill him, they might even save his life.

Adam's world narrowed to that moment. All he saw was the way out, and that was the cops at his front door. He turned to walk out—

But at that moment his body finally gave up on him. The body he had pushed to all its limits finally shuddered and stopped. Adam felt his heart jerk like that of a wounded rabbit and dropped to the floor with his eyes wide open.

CHAPTER 20

Detective Castle stood outside the door, his hand hovering over his holstered gun. His partner, Detective Murdock, was right behind him, his brow furrowed with concern.

"Something's wrong," Murdock muttered. He could feel it in his gut.

"I'm pretty sure someone is inside but they either didn't hear our call or chose to ignore it. I don't know which is scarier."

"Must be a cool customer," Castle said, "Let's say hi."

Castle gave the signal and Murdock shoved the door in with nothing but his shoulders and a grunt.

The detectives stepped into the house and scanned the empty living room—

Murdock whispered, "Did you hear that?"

Castle nodded, his jaw tight. He could hear it too—something faint, a sound coming from inside the bathroom.

"Yeah. It came from the bathroom."

They walked deeper into the house till they spotted the blood in front of the bathroom. They both stopped, Murdock nodded towards Castle to open the door.

Castle reached for the door, turning the knob slowly, cautiously. The door creaked open.

"Holy shit." Castle stopped short, his eyes widening

as he took in the scene in front of him. The bathroom was a butchery—blood smeared across the floor, the walls, the sink, bloodied clothes and towels litter the floor and a body slumped in a heap by the sink. Adam Stenson's body.

"Jesus Christ," Murdock breathed, stepping inside.

Adam was lying face down in a pool of his own blood, pale and motionless. His skin was a sickly shade of white, his lips blue. Blood dripped steadily from a wound on his hip, soaking through the towels he had tried to use to stop the bleeding. His chest didn't rise or fall. No signs of life.

"Check him!" Castle barked, snapping into action.

Murdock knelt down beside Adam, pressing two fingers against the side of his neck, feeling for a pulse. Nothing. He pressed harder, his own pulse quickening.

"He's not breathing," Murdock said, his voice tight. "No pulse."

Murdock sprang into action, his instincts taking over. He tilted Adam's head back, clearing his airway, quickly scooping out any fluid that might block his breathing. Once he was sure the passage was open, he laced his fingers together, positioned them over Adam's chest, and began compressions.

"One, two, three—"

Castle cursed under his breath as he yanked his radio from his belt. "Dispatch, Detective Castle. Requesting immediate EMS at 10788 Buttonwood Lake Drive. Male, approximately 30, unconscious, no pulse. Possible overdose. Advise on ETA. Over."

Murdock had already powered through thirty compressions when he paused to deliver two sharp breaths. He went right back to pressing down on Adam's chest, but there was no response. No flicker of life. Nothing.

Castle exhaled, then reached over, resting a firm hand on Murdock's shoulder.

"He's gone."

Murdock clenched his jaw, unwilling to accept it. He tried one more hard compression, his hands pressing deep into Adam's unmoving chest—then finally, reluctantly, he stopped. A slow, seething frustration built inside him. He had fought to bring men back before. This wasn't supposed to be another loss.

Castle extended an arm. Murdock, his face dark with anger, grabbed it and pulled himself up. His fists clenched at his sides, his breath unsteady.

Castle glanced around the wreckage of the apartment—the scattered vials, the syringes, the empty promises of strength lying among the filth.

"Looks like we know who's been supplying the juice around here," he muttered.

The apartment was now a crime scene. Yellow police tape marked the perimeter, and a group of forensic techs methodically cataloged the evidence, sealing away bottles, syringes, and vials into plastic bags.

Detective Castle stood at the kitchen counter, watching as two EMTs zipped up the black body bag that now contained Adam's body. The paramedics strapped it down to the stretcher and began wheeling it out of the apartment.

Castle sighed, shaking his head. "Another kid dead from this shit," he muttered. "It's always the same story. You think it'll make you stronger, but it just eats you alive."

"Poor kid. Steroids are just dirty shit." Murdock stopped short and took a second to compose himself.
He stared at the bloody bathroom, a hollow ache settling in his chest. Was this really the guy they'd been after the whole time? The thought left him feeling empty, as if the answers they'd chased so hard had slipped through their fingers.

Castle stood beside him, his arms crossed. He didn't say anything, just nodded in agreement. There wasn't much to say anymore. They'd seen this a hundred times before— addicts thinking they could beat the system, thinking they could pump themselves full of chemicals and come out the other side without a scratch. But it never worked out that way.

The sound of the stretcher rolling across the floor echoed through the apartment, followed by the heavy thunk of the door closing behind the paramedics. Adam was gone now, his body headed for the morgue.

"Where are they taking him?" Murdock asked, turning to one of the EMTs as they packed up their gear.

"Hollywood Memorial," an EMT replied, carefully removing his latex gloves and placing them in an evidence bag.

Castle sighed, rubbing the back of his neck.

"Someone should call his family."

Murdock nodded, already pulling Adam's phone from the evidence bag. He scrolled through the contacts, finding the number he was looking for. He stared at it for a moment, then glanced up at Castle.

"I guess it's my turn," Murdock said, holding the phone up.

Castle looked relieved.

Murdock pressed the call button, holding the phone to his ear. The dial tone buzzed for a moment before a soft, worried voice answered.

"Hello, Adam? How are you holding up honey?" The voice was warm, a woman's voice—Adam's mother.

Murdock took a deep breath, closing his eyes for a moment. This part never gets easier.

"Mrs. Stenson," Murdock said quietly, his voice firm but gentle. "This is Detective Murdock. I'm afraid I have some bad news about your son, Adam."

There was a long pause on the other end of the line. Murdock's throat tightened. "Ma'am... I'm sorry to have to tell you this, but your son Adam has passed away."

The silence on the other end of the phone stretched for what felt like forever. Then, suddenly, a sharp cry—a caterwaul—filled the air, so loud that Murdock had to pull the phone away from his ear.

"No! No! My baby!" Mrs. Stenson's voice cracked, raw with grief. "No, please! He can't be gone! Not Adam! Not my baby!"

Murdock winced, holding the phone a little further

away as her sobs grew louder, more desperate. He glanced over at Castle, who had heard every word. Castle's face was grim, his jaw clenched tight.

"I'm so sorry, ma'am," Murdock said softly, his voice barely above a whisper. "I'm so, so sorry."

Her cries continued, louder now, uncontrollable sobs that seemed to shake the air around them. Murdock could feel the weight of it, the crushing grief of a mother who had just lost her son. It pressed down on him, heavy and suffocating.

Mrs. Stenson stared into the phone in disbelief as it fell to the floor, her hand flying to her chest as though trying to catch her breath. Her knees buckled, and she leaned against the doorway for support.

"My baby! My Adam! Nooo!" She screamed.

Behind her, Mr. Stenson appeared, his tall frame looming in the background. His face was set in a grim line, his jaw tight as he stepped forward.

"What's going on!?" he asked, his voice rough, though there was a faint tremor beneath it.

"Adam is gone, Bob! Our baby is gone!" Mrs. Stenson was barely able to get it out, trying to find her breath between the sobbing.

Mr. Stenson's face drained of color. He stood frozen for a moment, the weight of those words causing him to age fifty years in front of her eyes. He swallowed hard, his eyes wide with disbelief.

"No" he finally said, his voice shaking. "That can't be true." He picked the phone up. "Hello?! Hello!?" But the detective had already hung up.

Mrs. Stenson let out a gut-wrenching wail, her hand flying to her mouth as she crumbled into her husband's arms. Her shoulders heaved as she wept, the sound of her anguish filling the air, breaking the silence of the once-peaceful neighborhood.

Mr. Stenson held her tightly, his face a mask of sorrow as he struggled to keep himself together. He closed his eyes, his breath coming in ragged gasps, but there was a fury brewing behind his grief. His grip tightened on his wife as she continued to cry, her fingers clutching his shirt.

"I told you!" Mrs. Stenson suddenly shouted. She pushed hard against him with her voice filled with pain and accusation. "I told you we should've never let him go! You kicked him out of the car Bob! You kicked your own son out of the car! We didn't even ask—" She couldn't finish her sentence, her sobs making her words incomprehensible.

Mr. Stenson winced, the accusation hitting him hard. He knew exactly what she was talking about. It had been a heated argument, the day they bailed Adam out of jail after his fight with George led to an arrest. He had been furious with Adam—furious with how out of control his life had gotten. On the drive back, they fought bitterly, and in a moment of rage, Mr. Stenson had pulled over, ordering Adam to get out of the car and find his own way home.

"Honey—" Mr. Stenson began, his voice low and filled with guilt. "I didn't know. You know I didn't mean it like that."

"You didn't know?" Mrs. Stenson's voice was shrill, her tear-filled eyes blazing with anger. "You kicked him out of the car! Our son, and you left him out there—like a dog!"

"I thought it was what he needed!" Mr. Stenson shouted back, his face flushed with shame. "He was spiraling! I didn't know... I didn't know it would come to this!"

They stood there, locked in their grief, their anger intertwining with their sorrow.

Later that afternoon, Mr. and Mrs. Stenson arrived at the morgue, the weight of the day etched into every step they took. Catherine still wore the same clothes from earlier—a cardigan that hung loosely on her frame and slacks wrinkled from hours of sitting and waiting. She had added a pair of oversized sunglasses, not to block the sun, but to shield her swollen, tear-streaked face from the world. A crumpled tissue was clutched tightly in one hand, while Bob's firm grip on her other arm kept her steady as they approached the heavy glass doors.

Just as they reached the entrance, Bob stopped abruptly, his shoulders stiffening as he turned to face her. "Catherine, you don't have to do this. I can—"

"I do have to do this," she interrupted, her voice sharp and trembling. Her chin quivered as she fought to steady herself. "He's my son, Bob. I need to see him. Now let's go."

Her voice cracked on the last word, but she straightened her back, brushing past him before the lump in her throat could betray her resolve. Bob exhaled heavily, his breath shaky as he fell in step beside her, his hand still on her arm.

The fluorescent lights inside the morgue buzzed faintly, casting a cold, sterile glow over the tiled floors and blank walls. The air smelled faintly of antiseptic, but beneath it lingered something heavier, something that made Catherine's stomach churn.

A man in a lab coat approached them, his expression carefully neutral, as if he'd done this a thousand times before.

"Mr. and Mrs. Stenson?" he asked quietly, his voice low and measured.

Mr. Stenson nodded stiffly, his hand gripping Catherine's arm as if afraid she might collapse.

"This way," the man said, leading them down a hallway that felt impossibly long. Each step echoed faintly, punctuating the tension hanging between them.

They reached a room with a metal table in the center, flanked by cabinets and cold, steel fixtures.

Catherine hesitated at the doorway, her breath catching in her throat. For a moment, she couldn't move, couldn't force herself to take another step.

"Are you sure?" Bob asked again, his voice soft now, almost pleading.

Catherine gave a sharp nod, wiping her eyes beneath the rim of her sunglasses before stepping inside. Her knees felt weak, but she willed herself to stay upright. She had to do this.

The attendant pulled back a thin white sheet, revealing their son's face. His features were tranquil, unnaturally peaceful, and Catherine could feel the sob rising in her throat. She let out a broken cry and stumbled forward, her trembling fingers reaching out to touch his face.

"Adam..." she whispered, her voice cracking. "Oh, my sweet boy..."

Bob stood a step behind her, silent and unmoving, his hands clenched at his sides. He wanted to cry, to scream, to rage against the unfairness of it all, but the sight of his wife crumpling beside their son's lifeless body left him frozen.

"I should have seen it," Catherine said through her tears, her hands shaking as she smoothed Adam's hair. "I should have known something was wrong. I should have done something, Bob."

"There's nothing we could have done," he managed, his voice hoarse and unconvincing.

Catherine shook her head violently, her grief spilling out in sharp gasps. "No! No, he was hurting, and we didn't see it. We didn't help him."

Bob stepped forward, placing a hand on her shoulder. "We loved him, Catherine. We did everything we knew how to do."

She turned to him, her sunglasses sliding down to reveal swollen, red-rimmed eyes. "Then why is he lying here? Why is our son dead?"

Bob couldn't answer. He just pulled her into his arms as she clung to him, sobbing into his chest.

The attendant quietly stepped out of the room, leaving them alone with their grief. The only sounds were Catherine's muffled cries and the distant hum of machinery, a sterile backdrop to the raw devastation of two parents saying goodbye to their child.

CHAPTER 21

Sara sat at her kitchen table, her fingers idly tracing the rim of a coffee mug. The faint hum of the refrigerator was the only sound in the quiet studio apartment. Her gaze drifted toward the stack of labeled boxes piled high in the living room, the cluttered chaos she had promised herself she'd unpack days ago. Instead, she sighed into her coffee, the weight of her thoughts anchoring her in place.

She was frustrated with herself. Deep down, she'd known for a long time that things with Adam were beyond repair, that the damage he had caused—both to himself and their relationship—had gone too far. But even now, after everything, she couldn't shake the lingering care she still felt for him, no matter how much she tried.

She knew it was that anger and hurt that nudged her to say yes when George suggested that he stop by Adam's place when she came to pack her stuff.

A part of Sara hoped they would be caught. And when she was, at that moment, she was oddly relieved. Adam had finally caught her. She was too weak to stop it or tell him, so she prayed he would find out.

Her phone buzzed on the table, jolting her from her thoughts. The screen lit up with the name Mrs. Stenson. Sara wiped the tears from her eyes, hesitating for a moment before finally picking up.

"Hi, Mrs. Stenson."

The voice on the other end sounded strained, punctuated by faint sniffling. Sara froze, her heart sinking.

Before she could respond, the weight of it all crashed over her. The thought of hurting Adam's family—the people who had welcomed her so warmly—was unbearable. A fresh wave of tears spilled over as she broke down, the guilt cutting deeper than ever. This wasn't just about Adam anymore. She had let them down too.

"I'm–I'm so sorry Mrs. Stenson, it has been so lonely this past year with Adam… I know you must hate me but—"

Mr. Stenson jumped on the phone interrupting her.

"Sara, this is Bob, can you come over? It's about Adam."

Sara froze. Her heart thudded loudly in her chest, her grip tightening around the phone.

"Adam? What happened? What did he do?" she whispered, her voice barely audible.

"We'd rather tell you in person." Bob softly responded.

"Just tell me Mr. Stenson—what did he do now?!" Sara replied hesitantly not wanting the answer.

Bob sighed, cleared his throat, "Adam passed away today. He was found in his apartment earlier this morning."

The room seemed to tilt, her head spinning as the words hit her like a freight train. Adam was dead? Her Adam? The man she had loved, fought with, cheated on, and tried to forget. Gone.

She opened her mouth, but no words came. Her mind couldn't catch up with the flood of emotions coursing through her.

"Sara, are you still there?" Bob's voice cut through the fog.

"I—I don't know," she stammered. "Are you sure? How… How did this happen?"

"Catherine would really love you here with us. If you can't drive I can pick you up."

"No— I'm—Thank you for letting me know," Sara

finally managed to say, her voice hollow. "I'll head over there shortly."

The call ended, leaving her in the deafening silence of her empty apartment. She stared at the phone in her hand, the reality of the situation slowly sinking in. Adam was dead, and all she could feel was an overwhelming mix of confusion. She had cried the last time she saw Adam because she knew that the man she once loved was gone. The sensitive and loving man she fell so quickly for. The kind, gentle Adam who had held her close on quiet nights, who had told her she was beautiful even when she didn't feel it—that Adam had disappeared, replaced by a selfish, steroid abusing man that she pitied.

Now, sitting at her kitchen table, Sara felt the weight of those memories crushing her. She hadn't been able to help him. She hadn't been able to save him from himself. And now it was too late. A tear slid down her cheek as she whispered to the empty room,

"I'm so sorry, Adam."

Her phone buzzed again, jolting her back to reality. It was George.

Had he heard the news? He was Adam's only friend so his number would be right beside hers probably. She hesitated before answering, knowing what he was going to say.

"Hey, Sara—I just heard—," George's voice was soft, almost hesitant.

Sara didn't say anything. She held her phone tighter in her grip and waited.

"I—How are you holding up?"

Sara swallowed hard, trying to keep her voice steady. "I— I don't know, George. I don't know how to feel."

"I think you should come down here. You shouldn't be alone right now and I'm the only person who understands what you are feeling."

Sara closed her eyes, fighting back the flood of emotions. She knew George meant well, but the thought of seeing him—of facing the man who had been part of the reason her relationship with Adam had fallen apart—was too much. The guilt was still too raw.

"I can't, George," she said quietly. "I just... I can't and I shouldn't."

There was a pause on the other end of the line before George spoke again.

"Don't do this Sara. We can be together now—"

"No George!" She interrupted him. "We should never have done what we did. We should never have started, we should never have been so cruel."

Sara's voice broke at the end as tears sprung free from her eyes.

"Don't say that!" George whispered furiously.

"You enjoyed every second of what he had. You enjoyed the risks and played along just fine. You know we have a spark that you and Adam didn't. I'm not even saying we should do or be anything. I'm saying let's be together right now, let's mourn Adam together. As the two people who knew him best."

None of it mattered anymore. Adam was gone, and no amount of guilt or grief would change that. Seeing George wouldn't stop the ache in her chest or the weight of regret pressing down on her.

Sara shook her head with tears streaming down her face even though George could not see her. She wasn't going to do this anymore. She had failed Adam already but would not go on to live like this.

"I don't want to see you and I don't want you to reach out to me anymore."

She ended the call and set the phone down, staring blankly at the wall in front of her.

"I'm doing this for us," Adam had told her one night, his eyes wide with excitement.

"I'm going to be bigger, stronger. I'm going to take care of you."

At first, she had believed him. She had supported him, even when she had her doubts. But as the weeks turned into months, Adam had become consumed by his obsession. His moods had darkened, his temper had flared, and Sara had found herself walking on eggshells around him.

Sara leaned back in her chair, her chest tightening with regret. She had cheated on him, and she had never truly forgiven herself for it. She had wanted to make things right, but Adam had been too far gone. Now, she would never get the chance.

She stood up, walking to the window and staring out at the street below. Life was still moving, people were still going about their day, but for Sara, time had stopped the moment she had heard Adam's name on the other end of that phone call. She wasn't sure how to move forward, how to process this grief, this guilt. All she knew was that a part of her had died with Adam that morning. And there was no going back.

CHAPTER 22

Sara sat in her car, the engine idling softly beneath her. The suburban streets outside were quiet, lined with rows of neatly trimmed hedges and identical mailboxes. But the world beyond her windshield was a blur, overshadowed by the weight of the news. She tightened her grip on the steering wheel, her knuckles turning white.

She glanced at the house in front of her—Adam's childhood home. A modest, two-story house with faded blue siding and a porch that sagged slightly with age. The flowers in the garden were wilting, much like the spirits of the people who lived inside. Mr. and Mrs. Stenson. Adam's parents.

She had always been polite with them, keeping a respectful distance out of fear that her rocky relationship with Adam might sour their opinion of her. But despite everything, they were kind people. They'd always tried to reach out, even when Adam became more distant. Mrs. Stenson had called often and invited her for lunch. She would spend the whole time asking how Adam was doing, concerned about his obsession with working out. Sara had always downplayed it, hoping it would eventually pass.

But now, sitting outside their house with the news of their only son's death, Sara felt like the weight of the world was pressing down on her chest. She swallowed hard, her throat dry and tight. She couldn't sit here forever.

With trembling hands, Sara turned off the engine, her heart pounding louder than the ticking of the cooling car. She stepped out, feeling the cold autumn air bite at her skin, pulling her coat tighter around herself as she walked up the driveway. The leaves crunched under her boots, and the sound felt deafening in the quiet neighborhood.

At the door, Sara hesitated, her hand hovering over the doorbell. Her fingers trembled as they pressed the doorbell, and she immediately heard the faint chime echo through the house.

Footsteps approached, and the door creaked open to reveal Mr. Stenson. His eyes were swollen, his face etched with grief, his shoulders slumped forward under an invisible weight.

Without a word, Sara collapsed into him, her head resting against his chest. His arms encircled her, and they clung to each other as she sobbed. The tears came harder this time, harder than when she first heard the news. Maybe it was the reality sinking in—seeing someone who shared her closeness to Adam, someone who felt the same unbearable loss.

"I should've said something," Sara murmured, her voice quivering, barely audible over the weight of her sorrow.

Mrs. Stenson appeared next, her movements slow and deliberate as she stepped forward. She paused near them, her presence fragile but resolute. Behind dark sunglasses, her voice cracked as she spoke.

"Hi, my love..."

The sight of her shattered Sara all over again. She broke away from Mr. Stenson's embrace and fell into hers. The two women held each other tightly, their grief spilling out in uncontrollable, gut-wrenching sobs.

"I'm so sorry," Sara choked out between her tears.

"I know, honey. We all are," Mrs. Stenson whispered softly, her words carrying both comfort and the weight of shared pain.

Sara slowly pulled away from her embrace.

"I knew about the steroids. I knew for months actually. I knew what he was doing to his body, but I didn't tell anyone. I thought he'd stop on his own. He promised me so many times that he would stop. I thought—"

Mrs. Stenson's tear-streaked face turned toward Sara, her eyes filled with a mix of grief and betrayal.

"Why didn't you tell us?"

"After the time at the hospital he went clean. He really stopped but relapsed shortly after and there was nothing I could do at that point to help him."

Sara swallowed hard, fresh tears spilling down her cheeks.

"I didn't want to upset you. I didn't want to make things worse between you and Adam. I thought Adam and I could handle it, but I was wrong."

For a moment, there was only silence. Mrs. Stenson's sobs quieted as the three of them stood there, bound together by their grief, their regret, their shared love for the man who was now gone.

"He was our only son," Mr. Stenson said finally, his voice hoarse, his eyes rimmed with tears he hadn't yet allowed to fall. "And now he's gone."

Mrs. Stenson leaned into her husband, her body trembling as she wept quietly into his chest. Mr. Stenson held her close, his hand stroking her back, though he, too, looked like he was barely holding himself together.

The three of them stood in the doorway, mourning together, bound by their love for Adam and the grief that had ripped their lives apart. There were no more accusations, no more anger. Only the heavy silence of loss.

Sara's heart felt like it was shattering into a million pieces as she watched them, her mind flooded with memories of Adam—of the man he had been, the man she had loved despite everything that had gone wrong between them.

"I miss him," Mrs. Stenson whispered, her voice raw with pain. "I miss him so much."

Mr. Stenson nodded, his eyes distant.

"So do I–"

Sara bit her lip, fighting back the sobs that threatened to overtake her again. She had never imagined it would end like this. She had never imagined that she would feel so much regret, so much pain, for all the things she hadn't said or done when she had the chance.

"I'm sorry," Sara said again, her voice breaking. "I'm so, so sorry."

Mrs. Stenson nodded through her tears, her hand reaching out to take Sara's in a gesture of shared sorrow.

"We'll get through this," she said, though her voice wavered with uncertainty. "Somehow, we'll get through this."

The sun had begun to set behind them, casting long shadows over the quiet street. And there, on the doorstep of the house that had once been Adam's home, they stood together, grieving for the man they had lost.

CHAPTER 23

The small church was quiet, save for the soft hum of the ceiling fan overhead. Light streamed through the stained-glass windows, casting muted colors across the rows of empty wooden pews. At the front of the room stood Adam's casket, lid open, surrounded by a few simple flower arrangements.

The service was small and somber, exactly as Adam's parents had requested. A scattering of family friends and a few distant cousins filled the quiet room, their murmured condolences blending with the soft strains of a hymn playing faintly in the background. They had all come to say goodbye to Adam—the boy they had lost long before his body gave out.

In the front row, Mr. and Mrs. Stenson sat hand in hand, their fingers interlocked tightly. Grief etched deep lines into their faces, their vacant stares fixed on the simple wooden casket draped in white lilies.

Sara sat beside them, her body heavy with exhaustion and heartbreak. Her eyes, puffy and bloodshot from days of crying, reflected by the sleepless nights she'd endured since hearing the news. She kept her gaze low, unable to look at the casket for too long without fresh tears threatening to spill.

The room felt stifling, the air thick with unspoken sorrow, as those gathered exchanged hushed words and sorrowful glances, each grappling with their own small piece of Adam's story.

George stood awkwardly in the back, shifting his weight from one foot to the other. He wore a muted black suit and a hat which he wore real low. His face was a mess. Adam had done a number on him and he still had the swelling and bruising to prove it.

The pastor, an older man with salt and pepper hair and a calm demeanor, stepped up to the podium. He cleared his throat gently, and began speaking in a soothing but firm voice.

"We are here today to say goodbye to Adam Stenson," he began, looking out over the small gathering. "A son, a friend, a lover. A young man whose life was cut tragically short."

He paused, glancing down at the casket, as if he too was mourning the loss of potential, the loss of someone who had strayed too far from who he once was.

Mrs. Stenson wept softly into her handkerchief, her shoulders trembling as her husband wrapped a strong arm around her in a steadying gesture. Beside her, Sara leaned her head gently against Mrs. Stenson's shoulder, fighting to keep her composure even as guilt gnawed relentlessly at her from within.

The pastor continued.

"Today is about remembering Adam. Remembering the person he was before—before things changed. I'd like to invite those who knew him best to come up and share a few things. Let us remember him as he was."

Mr. Stenson stood first, his movements slow and heavy and his face drawn tight. He approached the casket and stared down at his son's face, pale and cold, framed by the white satin lining. He hadn't seen Adam like this—so still, so quiet—in years. It took him a moment before he could speak.

"Adam, he wasn't always–," Mr. Stenson began, his voice rough, worn down by grief. His usual booming voice had lost its luster.

"I'll be speaking on behalf of Catherine as well—

She—," Mr. Stenson's voice cracking. "Just too much for her. Understandably." He cleared his throat again and wiped his tears. "Adam was quiet, shy even, but he had a good heart. He was fiercely loyal." He stopped, his throat tightening.

"When Adam was young, he used to stick up for the kids who got picked on and— and what was so special about that is most of those kids were bigger than him. He wouldn't say much, but if he saw something wrong, he couldn't just walk away. That was my boy."

The room was still as Mr. Stenson wiped at his eyes with the back of his hand.

"He was a good kid. And he loved his family. We all loved him, even when things started to change. Even when... Even when he wasn't the same anymore."

Mrs. Stenson broke down again, her sobs echoing softly in the small space. Mr. Stenson gave her a brief, pained glance before continuing.

"I don't know what made him start this downward spiral," he said, shaking his head slightly. "He cried for help and I was too dumb to see it. I didn't even know about what was going on until it was too late. But I could see the change in him. He wasn't our Adam anymore. I wanted to help him. We all did. But he wouldn't let us in. I'll miss my son, my best friend." Mr. Stenson looked down again at the casket. "I'm sorry I failed you son."

He stepped back from the casket, his hands trembling as he returned to his seat, pulling his sobbing wife close. The pastor nodded solemnly and gestured for the next person to come forward. Sara swallowed hard, knowing it was her turn when the pastor met her eyes with a knowing look. Her legs felt weak as she stood, her heart hammering in her chest. She walked slowly up to the casket, her hands shaking slightly as she gripped the edge of the podium for support.

"Adam—" she began, her voice barely above a whisper. "Adam was, he was my person. He was—kind and funny. When we first started dating, he was the nicest guy I'd ever met. Sort of quiet but I loved that about him. He was always looking out for me, always wanting to make sure I was okay."

She paused, her throat tight. "Back then he didn't care that he wasn't the biggest guy. He was just... Adam."

She closed her eyes for a moment, remembering the person he had been before everything went wrong.

"But things changed," she continued, her voice shaking now.

"I'll never forget the first time he ended up in the hospital. I was so scared when I saw him lying there, he looked so vulnerable. He said he'd change." She bit her lip, feeling tears burn behind her eyes.

"He did change but only for a while," she said softly. "Eventually, Adam went back and I— I lied. I lied to his parents. I lied to them for him, covered for him because he begged me to. I didn't want to see him in pain, but I should've known better. I'm so sorry." She looked over at Mr. and Mrs. Stenson, her voice breaking. "I'm so sorry."

Mr. and Mrs. Stenson's eyes glistened with tears, their grief etched into every line of their faces. Mrs. Stenson clutched her handkerchief tightly, as she looked at Sara. Mr. Stenson's jaw tightened, a silent attempt to hold himself together, but his red-rimmed eyes betrayed the storm of emotions swirling inside him. Then, slowly, they both nodded, their expressions a mixture of heartbreak and understanding. It wasn't forgiveness—at least, not entirely—but an acknowledgment of her words and the weight they carried.

There was a long, painful silence as Sara stood there, feeling the weight of her guilt crushing her from the inside out. "I always loved Adam and I'll never be the same now that he is—gone."

She wiped her eyes quickly and stepped down, unable to look at the casket as she passed it. She returned to her seat, her shoulders hunched, her face buried in her hands. Mrs. Stenson leaned over and hugged her tightly.

George shifted in the back of the room, his heart pounding in his chest. He didn't want to go up there. He didn't want to say anything. But he knew he couldn't avoid it. Not here. Not now.

He made his way to the front of the church, each step

echoing softly against the wooden floor. His movements were slow, almost reluctant, as if the weight of the moment pressed down on him. As he passed Sara and Mr. and Mrs. Stenson, he kept his gaze forward, unable to meet their eyes. He couldn't bear to see the pain written across their faces—it was too much.

He stopped in front of Adam's casket and stared down at his friend's face, pale and cold, so different from the Adam he remembered. A lump formed in his throat as he looked up at everyone there.

"Adam was my best friend," George began, his voice low and rough. "We met in high school and even though we were very different people we got along in the best of ways, we even worked together at this shitty telemarketing job for years." His hands trembled slightly as he gripped the edge of the podium. "Adam was a good guy. We had some good times... before all of this."

George paused, his eyes flicking over to Sara for a brief second. His stomach twisted with guilt. He thought about all the times Adam had almost caught him—him and Sara. He could still see the look on Adam's face that day, the rage, the betrayal.

"I messed up," George said, his voice barely above a whisper. He stared down at his feet, unable to meet anyone's eyes. "I made mistakes. And I'm truly sorry. Adam— you didn't deserve this."

He stepped back from the podium, feeling sick to his stomach. It wasn't a real apology, and he knew it. His guilt wasn't for what he'd done—it was for getting caught.

As George made his way to the back and sat down, the weight of his betrayal hung heavy in the air, unspoken but felt by everyone in the room.

After a few more people spoke—distant relatives and family friends, their words blending into a haze of memories and sorrow—the service drew to a close.

The pastor stepped up to the podium once more, offering a final prayer for Adam's soul and a few words of comfort for those left behind.

"Let us remember Adam for who he was," the pastor said quietly, his voice steady. "Not for the mistakes he made, but for the love he gave. For the lives he touched."

Sara's eyes were fixed on the casket, her heart aching. She couldn't stop replaying that day in her head—the day Adam had walked in on her and George. She remembered the look on his face, the shock, the anger. The way he had lunged at George, fists flying, screaming like an animal. She had never seen him like that before.

It was the steroids, she knew. They'd taken the Adam she loved and twisted him into something she couldn't recognize. But still, she couldn't escape the guilt. She had lied. She had betrayed him. And now, he was gone, and all she had left were regrets.

Mrs. Stenson looked over to her, her face etched with grief, but she nodded slowly. "I know," she whispered back, her voice hoarse from sobbing. "I know you loved him."

Sara hugged her tightly, tears streaming down her face. It wasn't enough, she thought. Nothing would ever be enough.

George watched from the back of the room, his heart heavy. He could see the pain in Sara's eyes, the way she was trying to make up for everything that had happened. But he knew the truth—there was no making up for what they had done.

The service ended quietly. One by one, the small group of mourners filed out of the church in twos and threes, leaving behind the casket, now closed, ready to be taken to the cemetery for burial.

Sara stood outside with Mr. and Mrs. Stenson, holding Mrs. Stenson's hand as they said their goodbyes to the people that came. George lingered in the background, watching from a distance, his hands shoved deep into his pockets. He couldn't bring himself to join them, to offer any real comfort. He couldn't even look them in the eye.

As the final guests left, Sara turned to Mr. and Mrs. Stenson, her voice soft.

"He was a good man," she said quietly. "Before everything, he was a good man."

Mrs. Stenson nodded, her eyes still wet with tears. "He was," she whispered. "He really was."

CHAPTER 24

Sara stood at the window of her small apartment, staring out at the street below. The world outside moved on—cars zipped by, people walked their dogs, mothers pushed strollers. It was a day just like any other, but for Sara, every day now felt like a small echo of grief.

She glanced down at her stomach, where her hand rested protectively over a slight swell that only she noticed. She was a few months along now, and the changes were beginning to show. But no one else knew—no one except her. And now every time she looked in the mirror, she was reminded of Adam.

The thought of him still sent a dull ache through her chest. It had been months since his death, but the pain hadn't faded. If anything, it had grown heavier, pressing down on her each day. She ran her fingers over her stomach absentmindedly, trying to ground herself. This is his child, she thought.

She hadn't told anyone. Not his parents, not her friends—no one. She wasn't sure why. Maybe it was fear, or guilt, or some twisted hope that keeping this secret gave her one last connection to Adam. It was the one piece of him she had left.

Her phone buzzed, pulling her from her thoughts. It

was a text from Mrs. Stenson. Sara's throat tightened.

Hi, Sara. Just checking in. Are you free to stop by today? We'd love to see you.

The Stensons had grown used to her visits, and in a way, she had too. It was another way of staying connected to Adam, even though the visits sometimes were painful. Sitting with his parents, seeing the grief in their eyes still, hearing the way Mrs. Stenson spoke about her son in the past tense—it never got easier. Sara stared at the message for a long moment before replying.

Yes. I'll be over this afternoon.

She set the phone down and leaned against the counter, her hand still on her stomach. When are you going to tell them? The thought gnawed at her constantly, but the words never came. Every time she was about to say something, she froze.

What would they think?

She didn't even know how she felt about it most days. Part of her was terrified—How can I do this alone? And another part of her, the part that couldn't let go of the past, was clinging to the idea that this baby would somehow bring Adam back. That through their child, she could find some kind of redemption.

She walked to the bedroom and opened the top drawer of her nightstand, pulling out the small ultrasound photo she kept hidden. She stared at it for a long time, her thumb tracing the blurry shape. A boy? A girl? Does it even matter? It was Adam's child. And that was all that mattered.

A couple miles away George sat hunched over his desk, staring blankly at his computer screen. The blinking cursor seemed to taunt him, daring him to get back to work, to pick up the phone and make another pointless call. But he couldn't focus. Not today. Not any day, really.

His fingers absently traced the scar above his eyebrow—the one Adam had left behind. It had healed, but the memory of that night still burned fresh in his mind. The night Adam caught him with Sara. The rage in his eyes, the sound of fists connecting with bone, the way he had barely made it out alive.

He closed his eyes, pressing his fingers harder into the scar, as if trying to erase it. But it was still there, just like the guilt that clung to him every single day.

"Yo, George!" A co-worker's voice broke through the haze. "We're hitting up Jerry's after work. You coming?"

George forced a tight smile.

"Nah, man. I'm good. I think I'll pass."

The co-worker raised an eyebrow.

"You've been good for weeks now, man. You used to be the guy dragging us all out for drinks. What happened?"

George shrugged, looking away.

"Just got a lot on my mind, I guess."

The co-worker studied him for a moment, then shook his head.

"Coo bro–just don't disappear on us completely."

George watched him walk away, feeling the familiar weight of guilt settle over him. He had already disappeared. The old George, the guy who used to laugh too loud, drink too much, and talk too big—he was gone. That George died the night Adam beat the life out of him.

He leaned back in his chair, rubbing his temples. The memory of Adam's fists—relentless, brutal—still haunted him, he had thought he was going to die. But what haunted him more was the betrayal. Adam was his best friend. And he had thrown it all away for her.

And now Adam was dead, and George was stuck here, in this dead-end job, living with the consequences, and Sara had moved on.

He was someone else now. Someone smaller. Someone trapped in his own skin, suffocating under the weight of regret and there was no way out.

Later in the evening, Sara sat on the couch in the Stenson's living room, watching as Mrs. Stenson poured tea. The house was quiet, except for the faint sound of a clock ticking in the hallway. It always felt like time moved slower here, like the grief that hung in the air weighed everything down.

Mrs. Stenson handed Sara the cup, her hands trembling slightly as she sat down beside her husband. They looked older now, more fragile. The loss of their son had aged them in a way that time itself hadn't.

"How are you, Sara?" Mrs. Stenson asked softly, her voice tinged with concern. "You've seemed a little distant lately."

Sara forced a smile, though it didn't reach her eyes.

"I'm okay," she lied. "Just busy with work, you know."

Mr. Stenson nodded, though his gaze was distant. "Work keeps the mind busy, I suppose. It's harder for us retired folks."

There was a long, heavy silence. Sara stared down at her cup of tea, her stomach twisting with guilt. Tell them.

The words were on the tip of her tongue, but they wouldn't come out. How could she tell them now? How could she drop this bombshell on them when they were still grieving?

Mrs. Stenson's voice broke the silence. "I was going through some of Adam's things the other day," she said quietly. "His old baseball cards, his drawings from school... it's still hard to believe he's really gone."

Sara's heart clenched. "I miss him too."

Mrs. Stenson reached out and took Sara's hand, her grip gentle but firm.

"He loved you, you know. He always talked about how lucky he was to have you."

Tears pricked at Sara's eyes, and she blinked them away quickly. "I loved him too."

There was so much more she wanted to say. How could she tell his parents that the baby she carried might be the last piece of their son left in the world?

Tell them. The words stayed stuck in her throat.

CHAPTER 25

Detective Murdock leaned back in his chair, his arms crossed, studying Erick like a puzzle he was determined to solve. Detective Castle, standing in the corner, tapped a pen against his palm, the rhythmic sound filling the tense room.

"So," Murdock began, his tone almost friendly, "Here's the thing, Erick. You've been around the block. You know the drill. Buying and using illegal steroids? That's not a slap on the wrist. We're talking big fines, jail time, the whole nine. But—" he leaned forward, lowering his voice, "—you help us find Jason, and maybe we can make some of this go away."

Erick stared at the table, his massive hands clasped together. He didn't flinch, didn't speak, didn't even blink.

Castle sighed dramatically, pushing off the wall.

"Alright, let's cut the crap," he barked, his voice booming. "Where is he?! You've been buying from him for years. Tell us and I'll do everything I can to get you off with just a warning."

Erick's jaw tightened, but he remained silent, his expression unreadable.

"Come on, Erick," Murdock tried again, softening his tone. "You're a smart guy. You know Jason's bad news. Help us, and we'll help you."

Still nothing.

Castle slammed his hand on the table, making the pen bounce. "Fine. You want to play tough? Let's talk about Adam Stenson. Ring any bells?"

At the mention of the name, Erick's eyes flicked up, a spark of confusion breaking through his stoic mask.

"Adam?" he asked, his voice low and gravelly. "What about him?"

Castle leaned in, his tone cold and deliberate. "We found him on his bathroom floor a few months ago. Bleeding out from a bad injection. His heart couldn't take it. Poor guy was clutching at his chest when he went down. Died alone, Erick. Alone and scared. And guess what? It was Jason's homemade shit that did it."

Murdock watched Erick closely as the words sank in. His face, once carved from stone, began to crack. He exhaled sharply, his hands clenching tighter.

"I didn't... I didn't know," Erick muttered, his voice heavy with remorse. "Adam... he delivered for Jason. He was just a young guy trying to find himself."

"Yeah," Castle snapped, "a guy who's now dead. And guess what? We can connect you to him. You're already in this, Erick. You think Jason's worth taking the fall for?"

Murdock leaned forward again, his voice low and urgent. "Help us find Jason. End this. Where is he, Erick? You know something."

For a long moment, Erick sat frozen, wrestling with his thoughts. Finally, he sighed, his shoulders slumping in defeat.

"There's... there's a shack," he said quietly. "On the outskirts. Jason bought it a few years back. Said he needed a place to lay low if things got hot."

Murdock and Castle exchanged a quick glance, their expressions unreadable. Castle nodded and pushed off the table.

"Good choice," Murdock said, standing up. "Let's hope it's not too late."

Moonlight cast eerie shadows across the peeling wood, and the wind howled through the surrounding trees, carrying the faint smell of damp earth and decay. Castle and Murdock parked their car a good distance away, stepping into the cold night air with their eyes scanning the surroundings.

"Looks like the kind of place where bad things happen," Murdock muttered, his hand resting on his holstered gun.

Castle nodded, his gaze fixed on the shack. "Let's do this carefully. Jason's a big guy. If he doesn't want to go quietly, we're gonna feel it."

As they approached, the wind kicked up, rattling loose pieces of the shack. Murdock knocked on the door, the sound echoing into the emptiness.

"Police! Open up!" he barked.

There was no response. Castle stepped to the side, peering into a cracked window, his hand signaling for Murdock to stay ready. Suddenly, a loud crash erupted inside, followed by the sound of glass breaking and hurried footsteps.

"He's bolting!" Castle shouted as Murdock kicked the door in.

The two detectives stormed inside, guns drawn. The room reeked of sweat and chemicals, the floor littered with empty vials, syringes, and crumpled bills. Jason stood in the middle of the room, his hulking frame illuminated by the dim light of a single dangling bulb. His girlfriend cowered in the corner, her eyes wide with fear.

"Freeze!" Castle shouted.

Jason didn't hesitate. With one swift motion, he grabbed a duffel bag and hurled it at Murdock, sending him stumbling backward. Then, like a charging bull, Jason barreled toward the back door, trying to make his escape.

"Stop!" Castle yelled, sprinting after him as Jason disappeared into the woods behind the shack. Murdock was right behind, his flashlight cutting through the darkness.

"Stop! Police!" Murdock yelled, but Jason kept running, his massive form surprisingly agile as he darted between the trees.

Castle pushed himself harder, the adrenaline surging through him. The sound of branches snapping and heavy breathing filled the forest. Jason was fast, but Castle was gaining.

Suddenly, Jason spun around and swung his elbow with incredible force, catching Castle square in the chest. The detective stumbled back, his breath knocked out of him. Jason didn't stop, following up with a shoulder charge that sent Castle sprawling to the ground.

"That's all you got?" Castle spat, rolling to his feet just as Jason lunged again.

This time, Castle ducked under Jason's swing and drove his shoulder into the big man's midsection, sending them both crashing into the dirt. Jason fought like a cornered animal, his fists pounding into Castle's sides, but Castle held on, grappling him into submission.

Murdock arrived just in time, slamming the butt of his gun into Jason's face to stop him from overpowering Castle. Together, they wrestled him onto his stomach, slapping handcuffs onto his massive wrists.

"You're done," Castle growled, breathing heavily as they hauled Jason to his feet.

Jason smirked, blood trickling from his lip. "You think this is over? You don't know shit."

Murdock looked toward the shack. "What about the girl?"

Castle shoved Jason. "We've got our man," he said coldly.

Back at the car, Jason sat cuffed in the back seat, his chest heaving but his face defiant. Castle leaned against the door, arms crossed, glaring at him.

"Strong guy like you, Jason," Castle taunted. "Didn't think you'd go down so easily."

Jason smirked, as his eyes darted side to side. "How'd you pigs find me?"

"There's no honor in your business," Murdock replied flatly. "People were eager to sell you out after what happened to Adam Stenson."

Jason's smirk wavered, but he quickly recovered, leaning back. "Adam?" he asked, feigning confusion. "Who's that?"

Castle's voice dropped, cold and sharp. "Who's that? Nice. You ain't that good of an actor."

Murdock got right into Jason's face. Nose to nose. "You didn't hear about your boy Adam? He bled out on his bathroom floor because of your shit."

Jason shrugged, though the tension in his jaw betrayed him. "That's on him. Couldn't handle the heat. Not my problem."

Murdock backed away, he had enough.

Castle's glare hardened, his fists clenching. "You think you're walking away from this?"

Jason smirked again, the cocky grin igniting Castle's simmering anger. With a burst of fury, Castle lunged at him, landing a solid punch across Jason's jaw.

Murdock quickly stepped in, grabbing Castle by the arms and pulling him back. "Castle, enough!" he barked. "Take it easy. We've got him."

Jason seized his moment. Easing himself out of the backseat, he lunged at Murdock with all his weight, slamming the detective to the ground. The impact knocked the wind out of Murdock, and Jason used the momentum to break into a full sprint toward the woods, his hands still cuffed.

He glanced back, a grin spreading across his face as he saw the distance he'd gained. For a brief moment, he thought he'd made it. Until—

The crack of a gunshot echoed through the night. Jason staggered, his grin freezing as blood bloomed across his chest. His eyes widened and his massive frame hit the ground, legs kicking reflexively before going still.

The crime scene was controlled chaos of flashing red and blue lights cutting through the night, illuminating the grim reality beneath. Yellow caution tape stretched across the area, fluttering in the cool breeze as officers methodically marked evidence with small numbered placards. A single streetlamp cast a harsh glow over the bloodstained pavement where the body had lain, now replaced by a darkened outline that seemed to hold the memory of violence.

Castle and Murdock stood in the cool night air, watching as the body bag was loaded into the ambulance. Castle shook his head, his fists still clenched.

"He should've rot in prison for what he did," Castle muttered, his voice thick with frustration. "I just couldn't let him escape this time..."

Murdock nodded, his breath visible in the cold. "You did what needed to be done, no jury, no trial."

He slapped him on the back. "We got him, partner."

For a moment, they watched in silence as the ambulance disappeared into the darkness. The night stretched out before them, heavy and still, leaving only the faintest sense of justice in its wake.

EPILOGUE

Sara sat on the edge of her bed, staring down at the ultrasound photo in her hands. It was blurry, barely distinguishable, but to her, it was everything.

She took a deep breath, her hand resting protectively on her stomach. She reached for her phone and scrolled through her contacts, stopping on Mrs. Stenson's name. Her heart pounded in her chest as she pressed the call button, listening to the phone ring.

On the third ring, Mrs. Stenson answered. "Hi Sara, is everything okay?"

Sara swallowed hard, her voice shaking. "Mrs. Stenson, there's something I need to tell you."

There was a pause on the other end of the line. "What is it, dear?"

Sara took a deep breath, her heart racing. No more secrets.

"I'm pregnant," she said softly. "And it's Adam's baby."

AUTHOR'S NOTE

Writing **Most Muscular** has been a deeply personal journey for me. This novel is based on the original script I wrote before it was adapted for the screen. While the film version took on a life of its own, I always felt that the soul of the story—the raw struggle, the psychological weight of chasing an impossible ideal—was lost in the process. There's a lot of opinions when it comes to filmmaking and the many people involved reshaped it into something different, something that no longer fully reflected the story I had originally set out to tell.

That's partly why I wanted to write this book. I needed to bring the story back to its roots, to explore the themes of **obsession, identity, and self-destruction** in a way that felt unfiltered and honest. While this is a work of fiction, I know the reality of these struggles is all too real for many people. The battle with body image, the need for validation, the endless chase for "better"—it's something I've witnessed firsthand, and I wanted to dive deep into that world without compromise.

If this story resonated with you, I'd love to hear your thoughts. You can reach out or follow my work at **onlychrislevine.com** or on social media with the handle **@onlychrislevine**

—Chris Levine

ABOUT THE AUTHOR

Chris Levine is an actor, screenwriter, and author whose passion for storytelling spans film, fitness, and fiction. Known for his roles in movies across multiple genres, he also wrote, produced, and starred in **Anabolic Life,** a film inspired by his background in bodybuilding. His latest novel, **Most Muscular,** is based on his original script before it was adapted for the screen, bringing back the raw, unfiltered themes of obsession, identity, and self-destruction.

Beyond **Most Muscular,** Chris has also written **Dinosaur Discoveries,** a children's book that blends adventure with learning, and **Jurassic Terrors,** a thrilling, graphic novel-inspired dinosaur story. Whether on screen or the page, his work continues to push boundaries, explore complex characters, and captivate audiences.

Printed in Great Britain
by Amazon

63195822R00109